Mia Kingtide

The Octopus' Gift

By Luke Kilpatrick

Book Cover by Luke Kilpatrick
Illustrations by Luke Kilpatrick

Fourth Paperback edition 2025

ISBN: 979-8-9924828-1-2

Luke Kilpatrick
luke@pitterpatterdiving.com
www.pitterpatterdiving.com

Table of Contents

For my daughter, Mia, whose wonder and curiosity reminds me of the endless mysteries of the ocean.

For my father, whose wisdom and encouragement guides me like a lighthouse in the darkest waters.

And for Jessica, my fiancée, whose unwavering love and support are the tides that propel me forward.

You each inspire me to explore, understand, and share the beauty of the ocean, one wave at a time.

- Luke Kilpatrick
January 2025

Chapter 1

The Octopus' Gift

It was one of those magical afternoons at Asilomar Beach in Pacific Grove, California, where the air smelled of salt and seaweed, and the waves sparkled like scattered diamonds under the sun.

The tide pools glistened like tiny, self-contained worlds, each brimming with color and life. Mia Kingtide hopped from rock to rock with the practiced ease of a young explorer, her GoPro camera in one hand and her waterproof notebook tucked under her arm.These afternoons were her favorite—just her, her dad, and the ocean. It was their tradition, these mini-adventures in nature's most intricate corners.

Each tide pool was alive with movement. Green sea anemones waved their delicate tentacles in the water, tiny shrimp darted between rocks, and crabs, startled by Mia's shadow, scuttled into crevices for cover.

Mia crouched down by a particularly large pool, the sun warming her back. The surface shimmered like a mirror, distorting the treasures hidden beneath. She leaned closer, her eyes widening as a swirl of reddish-brown and cream moved gracefully under

Nestled among the rocks was an octopus, its body pulsating with soft waves of color as it tried to squeeze under a ledge. Its tentacles curled and uncurled, as if deciding whether to hide or stay.

"Dad! Come quick! There's an octopus!" Mia yelled, her excitement bubbling over. Her dad was a little way down the shore, adjusting his camera to capture the waves crashing against the rocks. "That's amazing, Mia! Just be careful, alright?"

"I'm fine, Dad!" she called back, her voice brimming with excitement. But before he could reach her, a group of older kids wandered over. They spotted the octopus and crowded around, their laughter echoing off the rocks.

"Look at that thing!" one of them said, jabbing a finger toward the pool. "Let's get it out!" another chimed in, picking up a stick. Mia's heart sank as the kids leaned in, their shadows falling over the water. "Stop it!" Mia shouted, leaping to her feet. The kids turned to her, their faces a mix of amusement and annoyance. "What's your problem?" one sneered.

"You're scaring it!" Mia snapped, her voice trembling but firm. "It's not 'just an octopus.' They're smart, and you're hurting it!" The kids exchanged glances, muttering under their breath. After a moment, they shrugged and wandered off, tossing the stick aside.

Mia knelt back down, her chest tight as she watched the octopus thrash and writhe, trying to wedge itself further under the rock. Its colors were muted now, its body pulsing with fear. "It's okay," Mia whispered softly. "I'll help you." The rock trapping the octopus in the tide pool was large, its jagged edges partially embedded in the sand. Mia braced her hands against it and pushed with all her strength. The rock shifted slightly, but not enough.

"Come on," she muttered through gritted teeth, her arms straining. She tried again, her fingers slipping on the wet surface. The octopus seemed to sense her effort, its movements slowing as it waited. Finally, with one last push, the rock rolled just enough to create a gap. The octopus hesitated, its body trembling, and then, with a sudden burst of movement, it darted out of the pool and into the open water, vanishing in a puff of foam.

Mia collapsed onto the rocks, her arms aching but her heart soaring. "Good luck out there," she whispered. As the waves gently lapped at the edges of the tide pool, Mia was about to stand up when a flicker of movement caught her eye. She froze, her breath catching.

The octopus was back.

It emerged slowly, its tentacles undulating with a calm, deliberate grace. Mia's heart pounded as it glided closer to her. "Hey, little guy," she murmured. "What are you doing back here? I thought you were off to explore the ocean." The octopus moved with purpose, drawing nearer. In one of its tentacles, it held something — a small, shimmering object that sparkled in the sunlight. Mia's breath hitched as it stretched out its tentacle, offering the object to her. She hesitated, her hands trembling as she slowly reached out. The octopus gently placed the object in her palm.

Mia gasped. It was a shell unlike any she had ever seen. Its surface shimmered with an iridescent glow, shifting between deep blue, sea green, and golden light. The colors seemed to ripple, as though the shell held the essence of the ocean itself.

"Whoa…" she whispered, her voice barely audible. The octopus lingered for a moment, its large, intelligent eyes meeting Mia's. It was as if it were trying to tell her something, something beyond words. Gratitude? Trust? A message?

"Thank you," Mia said softly, her voice thick with emotion. The octopus bobbed slightly in the water, almost like a nod, before swirling away and disappearing into the waves.

Mia stared at the shell in her hand, feeling its warmth and the faint tingling sensation spreading through her fingers. It was as if the shell was alive, humming with some kind of unseen power.

"What just happened?" she murmured.

Her dad's voice broke the spell. "Mia! Time to head back!"

Mia stood, cradling the shell in her palm as she hurried over to where her dad was waiting. "Dad! You won't believe what just happened!" she exclaimed, holding out the shell for him to see. Her dad raised an eyebrow, examining it closely. "That's… incredible, Mia. Where did you get this?"

"The octopus gave it to me," she said, her voice brimming with awe. Her Dad, Luke chuckled. "An octopus gave you a shell? Sounds like a fairy tale."

"I'm serious!" Mia insisted. "I helped it, and then it came back and gave me this!" Her dad studied her face, his expression softening. "Well, if that's true, then it sounds like that octopus knew exactly who to thank."

Mia smiled, clutching the shell tightly. She didn't know how or why, but deep down, she knew this shell was special.

As they walked back along the beach, the sun began to dip toward the horizon, casting the sky in hues of orange and pink. Mia glanced back at the tide pools, her heart full of wonder and excitement.

She didn't know it yet, but her life was about to change forever.

Chapter 2

A Connection to the Ocean

Mia couldn't stop thinking about the octopus and the shell. The faint tingling in her hands hadn't fully faded, as if some of the magic had seeped into her skin and remained there. On her nightstand, the shell pulsed softly with a glow that seemed alive, casting ripples of shimmering light onto the walls of her room. It reminded her of sunlight dancing on the surface of the ocean, mesmerizing and endless.

She lay in bed, her mind a whirl of questions. Why had the octopus chosen her? Why give her this shell? Was it some kind of magical coincidence, or did the gift hold a deeper meaning?

She reached over and picked it up again, running her fingers along its surface. The colors swirled and shifted beneath her touch, deep blues, vibrant greens, and streaks of gold that seemed to ripple like waves. The shell felt warm, almost alive, and holding it filled her with a strange sense of calm.

Mia closed her eyes, hugging the shell to her chest. "What are you?" she whispered, her voice barely audible in the quiet room.

The shell didn't answer, of course. But as she drifted off to sleep, a faint sound broke the stillness, a soft, rhythmic bubbling. Mia's eyes shot open. The sound was faint but distinct, like the melodic gurgle of water. She sat up in bed, her heart pounding. "What is that?" she whispered to herself.

Her gaze darted around the room, landing on her fish tank. The soft hum of the water filter had always been a comforting background noise, but this was different, louder, almost… purposeful.

She swung her legs out of bed and tiptoed toward the tank. Her breath fogged the glass as she leaned closer, peering into the water. Inside, her goldfish, Sunny, swam in lazy circles, his orange scales glowing faintly in the light of the shell on her nightstand.

Mia was about to turn away when the sound came again, louder this time, a bubbling, melodic rhythm. And then a voice.

"Thank you for the food," the voice said

Mia gasped and stumbled backward, her hands flying to her mouth. "Who… who said that?" she stammered.

Sunny paused mid-swim, turning to face her. His round, black eyes seemed to lock onto hers with an intensity she had never noticed before.

"You can understand me?" he asked, his voice soft and curious.

Mia's heart stopped. "What? Wait… what?" She pointed a trembling finger at the tank. "Did you just, did you just *talk*?"

Sunny bobbed up and down, which Mia could only interpret as a nod. "I suppose I did. Though I've always been able to talk. You've just never listened before."

Mia's jaw dropped. She backed away, nearly tripping over her desk chair. "This is crazy. I'm going crazy," she whispered, shaking her head.

"It's not crazy," Sunny said cheerfully, swimming closer to the glass. "It's special. You're different now."

Mia sank onto her bed, still staring at the tank as though it might explode. Her mind raced, trying to make sense of what was happening. "I can't believe this," she muttered. "I'm talking to my fish. My *fish* is talking to me."

Sunny flicked his tail, his tone light and matter of fact. "It's not so strange. Lots of creatures have things to say. You just never noticed before."

"But why now?" Mia asked, her voice shaky. "Why can I understand you all of a sudden?"

Sunny twirled in the water, his fins fluttering. "It's the shell," he said simply. "There's something about it, something connected to the ocean. And now, so are you."

Mia glanced at the glowing shell on her nightstand, her fingers tingling again at the memory of holding it. "The shell," she murmured.

"It's not just a shell," Sunny continued. "It's a gift. The ocean chose you, Mia. It saw something in you, something special."

Mia's brow furrowed. "But why me? I'm just

a kid. I don't know anything about magic or… or talking to fish."

"You care," Sunny said simply. "That's enough."

Mia stared at the tank, her thoughts tumbling over each other like waves crashing on the shore. Was Sunny right? Was the shell really a gift, a bridge to a deeper connection with the ocean?

After a long pause, Mia stood and crossed to her nightstand. She picked up the shell again, its warmth seeping into her palm. The glow seemed to brighten, as if responding to her touch.

"Okay," she said softly, turning back to Sunny. "If this shell connects me to the ocean, what does that mean? What am I supposed to do with it?"

Sunny tilted his head—or at least, he moved in a way that made it seem like he was thinking. "Maybe it means you're supposed to help. The ocean needs someone to listen, someone to care."

Mia frowned, her grip tightening on the shell. She thought of the octopus, the way it had looked at her with those intelligent, trusting eyes. It had needed her help, and she had given it without hesitation.

"Help how?" she asked. "What can I do?"

Sunny swam in a slow circle. "Start by listening. The ocean has a lot to say, and now you can hear it. That's a good place to begin."

Mia nodded slowly, her heart pounding with a strange mix of fear and excitement. The shell hummed faintly in her hand, as if agreeing.

The rest of the night passed in a blur. Mia sat by the tank, talking to Sunny until her eyes grew heavy and she could no longer keep them open. When she finally climbed back into bed, the shell rested on her nightstand, its glow illuminating the room like a gentle nightlight.

As she drifted off to sleep, one thought echoed in her mind: *The ocean needs me.*

The next morning, Mia woke with the shell still glowing faintly. The events of the night felt like a dream, but the warmth of the shell in her hand reminded her that it was real. She didn't know what lay ahead, but she felt certain of one thing, her connection to the ocean had only just begun.

Chapter 3

Pool Time

Mia woke up feeling more curious than ever. The shell sat on her nightstand, its glow dimmer in the morning light but still mesmerizing. As she and her dad packed their bags for a trip to the Monterey Sports Center, she tucked the shell into her backpack.

The Sports Center was one of Mia's favorite places. The indoor pool was bustling with activity, filled with kids splashing, diving, and racing each other. The air was thick with the scent of chlorine and the sound of laughter.

"Ready to practice your free diving?" her dad asked as they set their bags down by the bleachers.

Mia grinned. "Definitely!"

She tugged on her mask and fins and hurried to

the pool. As soon as her feet hit the water, she felt it again, that sense of belonging, as if the water was welcoming her home.

She began with a simple dive, sliding smoothly into the water. Something about being underwater felt different today, effortless, natural. She swam the length of the pool, her strokes cutting cleanly through the water, but what struck her most was how long she could stay under. Normally, her lungs would start to burn after a few seconds, but this time, there was no discomfort at all.

Curious, Mia dove to the bottom of the deep end. The tiles were cool beneath her fingers as she crouched there, waiting for the familiar urge to surface. But it never came.

"Whoa," Mia whispered, bubbles escaping her lips. She froze, realizing she had just spoken underwater, and it had felt completely normal.

She stayed there for several minutes, watching the other swimmers from below. The noise of the pool faded into the soothing hum of the water. Everything felt calm, like she was in a world all her own.

As she swam toward the far end of the pool, something extraordinary happened. A small school of fish darted past her, fish that shouldn't have been there. They shimmered faintly, their scales glowing a soft blue as they moved in perfect harmony.

Mia blinked, wondering if she was imagining things. "Where did you come from?" she whispered.

To her astonishment, one of the fish turned and swam toward her. "We came to visit," it said in a high-pitched, sing-song voice. "You have the gift now."

Mia's heart raced. "The gift?"

"You're connected to the ocean," the fish replied. "You can understand us, and you can stay down here as long as you like."

Mia opened her mouth to ask more questions, but before she could, the fish darted away, disappearing into the shimmering light of the pool. She surfaced, her mind buzzing with possibilities.

As the afternoon wore on, Mia couldn't stop testing her limits. She swam faster than ever, gliding through the water like she was born to it. At one point, during a casual race with her friends, she beat everyone by an impressive margin.

Then, something even stranger happened. A stray pool noodle floated toward her, and without thinking, Mia raised her hand. The noodle stopped mid-drift, hovering in the air for a moment before dropping back into the water.

Mia's cheeks flushed with excitement and nerves. "Okay, that's definitely not normal," she muttered.

She glanced around to see if anyone had noticed. One of the lifeguards was watching her, his expression curious. Mia quickly smiled and adjusted her mask, hoping to look as ordinary as possible.

When it was time to leave, Mia couldn't keep her secret any longer. As she and her dad walked back to the car, she blurted out, "Dad! Something weird is happening to me!"

Her dad looked puzzled. "What do you mean, Mia?"

"I can hold my breath underwater forever! And I think I talked to a fish! Oh, and I can move things without touching them!"

Her dad chuckled. "That's quite the imagination you've got, Mia."

"No, I'm serious!" she insisted. "It all started after the octopus gave me that shell."

Her dad paused. He had seen the shell, its faint glow, its shifting colors. There was something undeniably magical about it.

"Maybe it's time we talked about what these abilities mean," he said gently. "If this is real, Mia, it's important you use these gifts wisely. These powers sound incredible, but they also sound like a big responsibility."

Mia looked down at the shell in her hands, its surface warm and glowing faintly. She didn't fully understand what was happening, but one thing was clear: her life had changed forever.

Chapter 4

Friends Beneath the Waves

The waters of Monterey Bay shimmered with the morning light as Mia Kingtide paddled her kayak through the calm waves. The air was crisp, carrying the salty tang of the ocean, and the rhythmic splash of her paddle against the water was soothing. This was one of her favorite places in the world, not only because of its beauty but also because of how alive it felt. She had been coming out here more and more often lately, ever since the octopus gave her the magical shell that changed her life.

Today, though, felt different. There was something about the bay, something alive and buzzing just beneath the surface. She could feel it, a faint hum, as though the ocean was calling to her.

A little further out, her dad, Luke, stood at the helm of *Pitter Patter*, their family boat. He kept an eye on Mia's kayak as it glided toward the kelp forest. "Remember to stay near the edge of the forest," he called over the VHF radio. "I'm keeping watch from here, but give me a call if you need anything."

"Got it, Dad!" Mia replied into the handheld VHF clipped to her life jacket. She glanced back at the boat, the sight of it comforting. Her dad's watchful eye gave her confidence to explore, but she also knew he trusted her to handle herself.

"All right, let's see what the day has in store," Mia said aloud, resting her paddle across the kayak. She leaned over the side, peering into the clear water.

That's when she saw him.

A sleek harbor seal popped his head above the surface, his round, dark eyes locking onto hers with unmistakable curiosity. His whiskers twitched, and he let out an excited bark before diving underwater and surfacing again, this time closer to her kayak.

"Hello there!" Mia said, leaning over.

The seal tilted his head and barked again, this time in a way that Mia could understand. "Are you Mia? The human who can talk to us?"

Mia's heart leaped. "I guess I am! How do you know about me?"

"Oh, word travels fast in the bay," the seal said, spinning in a circle. "I'm Flip! I've been wanting to meet you."

Before Mia could respond, there was a loud splash behind her, and she turned just in time to see a playful sea lion leap out of the water and twist mid-air before landing with a splash.

"Did someone say 'Mia'?" the sea lion called, her voice high-pitched and full of energy. She swam up to the kayak, bobbing up and down. "I'm Luna! I've been looking for you too! Flip said you're the human who actually listens to us."

Mia laughed. "I guess I am! It's nice to meet you, Luna."

A moment later, a small, furry face appeared above the water. The otter floated on his back, holding a clam in his paws. "I'm Marlow," he said calmly, his voice quieter but no less friendly. "I don't normally bother with humans, but you seem… different."

Mia felt warmth spread through her chest. "It's nice to meet all of you. I've never had animal friends before!"

"Well, get ready, because we've got a problem," Flip said, suddenly serious.

Flip, Luna, and Marlow swam closer, forming a little circle around Mia's kayak.

"There's something wrong near the Aquarium Intakes," Flip said, his tone urgent. "An old, deflated life raft is stuck down there, and it's a mess. It's trapped a bunch animals because it is coved in old fishing lines and nets. This whole mess is getting all tangled around the intakes!"

Luna nodded, her eyes wide. "We tried to move it, but it's too heavy for us. And the crabs tangled in it are not happy, they're pinching everything in sight!"

Marlow floated closer, his voice thoughtful. "If the raft stays there, it could damage the intake pipes. Those pipes bring water into the Monterey Bay Aquarium to keep the animals there alive. It's really important they stay clear."

Mia frowned, thinking about what they had said. She knew the intakes were part of the bay's marine protected area, meant to shield the ecosystem from harm. They sat about 60 feet below the surface and pulled in cold, nutrient-rich seawater that kept the aquarium's tanks healthy and full of life. But if the old life raft had been blown into the area during a storm, it could cause serious damage to the intakes, and the delicate ecosystem around them.

"I'm going to help," Mia told them, then picked up her VHF radio and called her dad.

"Dad, I'm heading toward the Aquarium Intakes. There's an old life raft tangled in the kelp and the intake pipes. It's a mess, and I need to get it out before it causes more damage."

Luke's voice came back immediately, calm but concerned. "Okay, but be careful. Those pipes are deep, and I don't want you diving too far. I'll stay here in *Pitter Patter* and keep an eye out. Let me know if you need anything."

"Thanks, Dad. I've got my friends with me," Mia said, glancing at Flip, Luna, and Marlow.

Luke chuckled. "I don't know what I'd do if I had a harbor seal, a sea lion, and an otter on my crew. Good luck, Miss Mia."

With Flip, Luna, and Marlow leading the way, Mia paddled toward the yellow marker buoys signifying the aquarium intakes. She knew this area well, it was protected by strict rules to keep it safe, but storms sometimes swept debris into the zone.

The tall, swaying fronds of giant kelp rose from the depths like an underwater forest, their golden tips catching the light just below the surface. As they approached, Mia could see the problem clearly.

A float attached to a net tangled in life raft bobbed on the surface, between the large yellow marker buoys, but Mia knew the real trouble was below. She tied her kayak off on to the kelp and prepared herself for the effort to come.

Mia put on her fins, and dive mask, securing her shell, radio and camera in a green bag she secured across her body and waist. She then slipped into the water, her wetsuit shielding her from the sharp chill of the Pacific. The world below the surface opened up before her, an eerie, magical realm of swaying kelp and filtered sunlight. Flip, Luna, and Marlow stayed close, their movements graceful and purposeful. Though she felt confident with her new marine friends nearby, the sight of the tangled life raft wedged against the intake pipes filled her with unease.

The pipes were massive, their metal surfaces weathered by years of ocean currents. Kelp fronds wrapped around the raft like a net of their own, while the tangled fishing nets posed a hazard to anything that ventured too close. The steady hum of the aquarium's intake system vibrated faintly through the water, a reminder of the critical role these pipes played in sustaining the creatures at the Monterey Bay Aquarium. The raft's position near the pipes made the situation even more precarious.

"I'll free the fish," Luna said, darting toward the mesh. Her sleek body twisted and turned as she carefully nosed her way around the tangled nets and fishing line, her agility allowing her to avoid the sharp hooks.

"I'll check where the ropes and material from the raft is wedged," Flip added, diving toward the base of the pipes. His strong, streamlined body moved with precision as he examined the way the raft had been forced into place by the storm.

Marlow floated closer to the raft, staying near the sea floor where the crabs scuttled in nervous circles. His calm voice carried through the water. "Stay still, everyone. We're going to get you out. No pinching, okay?" He gave one particularly angry crab a knowing look.

Mia swam closer to the trap, her heart pounding as she took in the full extent of the mess. Using her levitation powers, she focused on the tangled ropes first. Slowly, she lifted one rope at a time, untangling them from the raft's tangled netting and the kelp's delicate fronds. She worked methodically, she didn't worry about tearing the kelp as it grows at almost a foot a day and would be quickly replaced. Mia knew that giant kelp was a key part of the ecosystem, providing food and shelter for countless marine creatures. Even the small pieces she was breaking off would feed something.

Suddenly, Flip surfaced, his eyes wide with alarm. "Mia, there's something else!"

"What's wrong?" Mia asked, her pulse quickening.

"The raft isn't just caught on the pipes, it's snagged on one of the intake grates. And the current from the intake is pulling harder than it should. It's trying to suck in the raft!"

Mia's stomach dropped. The intake pipes had powerful suction to draw in seawater for the aquarium, but if the rubber from raft got pulled into the system, it could cause severe damage, not just to the pipes, but to the animals relying on the water. Worse, the suction was creating strong currents that could pull in anything, or anyone who got too close.

"I'll hold it steady!" Flip shouted, diving back down to press his body against the trap and keep it from shifting.

"Be careful, Flip!" Mia called after him, her voice tinged with worry.

Luna swam to Mia's side, her playful demeanor replaced by a focused intensity. "We have to move fast. The current's getting stronger." Mia nodded, her mind racing. She gripped the glowing shell in her pocket, feeling its warmth spread through her hand. "Okay, Luna, keep freeing the fish. Marlow, get the crabs out. I'll focus on loosening the raft from the grate."

Mia swam closer to the intake pipes, the hum of the machinery growing louder as the current tugged at her. The raft shifted slightly, as if the suction were trying to claim it. Flip strained against the raft, his body acting as a barrier between it and the pipes.

"Hurry, Mia!" Flip barked. "I can't hold it much longer!" Mia took a deep breath, steadying her nerves. She focused her levitation powers on the raft, lifting it just enough to reduce the pressure on the ropes. The raft groaned as it moved, the rubber protesting her efforts.

Luna worked quickly, nudging the last trapped fish through a gap in the netting. "You're free! Go, go, go!" she urged, her voice urgent but encouraging.

Meanwhile, Marlow had coaxed most of the crabs out from under the raft. One particularly stubborn crab refused to budge, snapping its claws defiantly. "Come on, buddy," Marlow said, his tone patient but firm. "This isn't the place for a standoff."

Marlow finally managed to guide the crab out, just as Mia felt the raft shift dangerously under her control. The suction from the intake pulled harder, and the raft pulled toward the pipes, threatening to swallow it.

"I need help!" Mia cried, her arms trembling as she tried to keep the raft steady with her powers.

Luna darted toward her. "I'll push from below!" The sea lion positioned herself beneath the raft, using her strong flippers to hold it steady. Flip, still bracing the raft from the side, grunted with effort. "We've got this! Just a little more!"

Mia gritted her teeth, pouring all her focus into lifting the raft. The shell in her pocket seemed to glow brighter, filling her with a renewed surge of strength. Slowly, the raft began to rise, inch by inch, away from the intake grate.

With one final push, the raft broke free from the pipes. Mia and her friends worked together to guide it to the surface, where she secured it to her kayak with ropes. The tension in her chest eased as she saw the raft safely at the surface and not endangering anything deeper in the water.

"You did it!" Flip exclaimed, his voice full of relief. "We all did," Mia said, her heart still pounding. She glanced at Luna, who was playfully splashing near the surface, and Marlow, who floated on his back with a satisfied grin.

The kelp swayed gently around them. The intake pipes hummed quietly, their protective grates free from obstruction. The bay felt peaceful again, as though it had taken a deep breath of relief.

As Mia paddled back toward Pitter Patter, her dad's voice crackled over the VHF. "Mia, everything okay out there?"

"Mission accomplished, Dad," Mia replied, her voice light with triumph. "The raft is behind my kayak, and the intakes are clear."

"Good work, Miss Mia, paddle out of the kelp a bit and we can load it up on *Pitter Patter* and have it disposed of properly" Luke said. She could hear the pride in his voice.

Flip, Luna, and Marlow swam alongside her, their laughter and playful splashes filling the air. Mia glanced down at the glowing shell in her pocket, a smile spreading across her face.

"I promise," she said softly, "I'll always do my part to protect the ocean. No matter what."

From the water, Flip barked in agreement. "We're with you, Mia. Always."

Mia smiled, her connection to the sea, and her new friends, stronger than ever.

Chapter 5

The Mysterious Whale Song

The sun had just begun to rise over the jagged cliffs of Big Sur, painting the sky in hues of orange and pink. Mia Kingtide stretched in the berth on *Pitter Patter*, as the gentle motion of the waves rocked her awake. She and her dad had spent the night anchored in a quiet cove, ready to dive at a special site called Flintstones.

"Morning, Mia," her dad called from the helm, a cold can of sugar free Red Bull in his hand. "Ready to explore the underwater world today?" "Always!" Mia replied, already pulling her wetsuit from its hook.

Flintstones was a legendary dive spot, known for its towering underwater rock formations and abundance of sea life. Mia and her dad had been planning this trip for weeks, eager to capture photos of the vibrant ecosystem below. As they prepared their gear, a deep, haunting sound cut through the morning air.

Mia froze, her mask halfway to her face. "Dad, did you hear that?" Her dad lowered his Red Bull can, his brow furrowing. "That's a whale song. And it doesn't sound right."

The sound came again, louder and even more mournful. "Something's wrong," Mia said, her heart sinking.

They quickly stowed their dive gear, pulled up the anchor, and motored toward the sound. The *Pitter Patter* cut smoothly through the water, its diesel engine humming softly. As they drew closer, the calls grew more frequent, filling the air with a sense of urgency.

Mia scanned the horizon, her sharp eyes catching a flash of movement. "There!" she shouted, pointing. A young humpback whale floated near the surface, its movements sluggish and labored. As they approached, Mia's stomach twisted.

"It's tangled," she whispered. Thick ropes from crabbing gear wrapped tightly around the whale's tail and pectoral fins, cutting into its flesh. Large floats bobbed around it, weighing the whale down with every attempt to move.

Humpback whales were no strangers to Mia. She knew they were some of the most incredible creatures in the ocean, migrating thousands of miles each year between their feeding grounds in the cold waters of the Pacific and their breeding grounds in Hawaii. This young whale should have been well on its way to warmer waters by now, joining a pod on the long journey to the islands.

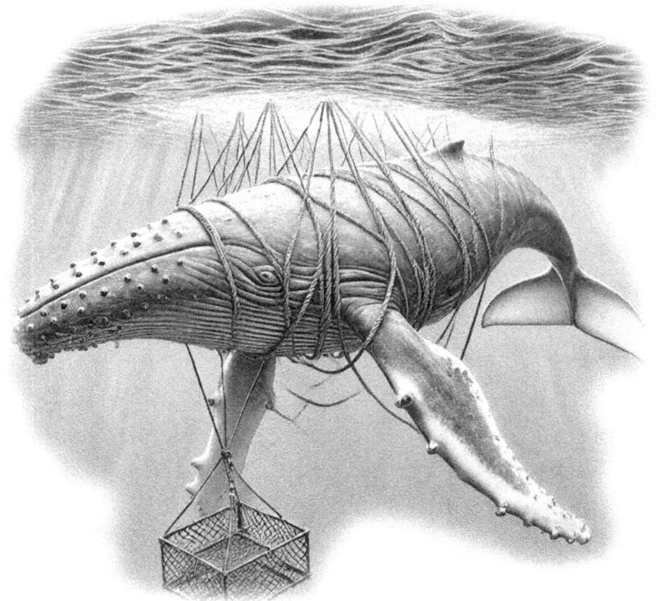

"These whales are amazing, Dad," Mia said softly, her voice tinged with sorrow. "They help balance the ocean ecosystem, moving nutrients between the surface and the deep when they dive."

"And they're in danger because of this mess," her dad replied, gesturing toward the tangled ropes.

Crabbing gear like this was a known hazard to marine life. Despite recent advancements in ropeless traps, devices that use GPS and remote-release technology to retrieve traps without leaving ropes in the water, many crabbers still used traditional gear.

"This is why we need more people to switch to ropeless traps," Luke said. "They'd prevent so many entanglements like this." Mia and her dad worked quickly, grabbing a pair of heavy-duty scissors, an underwater saw, and a safety line.

"Ready to help, Mia?" her dad asked, his voice steady but serious. Mia nodded. "I can talk to it, Dad. I'll let it know we're here to help."

They dropped anchor, then together, they slipped into the water. The cold Pacific wrapped around them, but Mia barely noticed. Her focus was on the struggling whale ahead. Underwater, the scene was heartbreaking. The young humpback's massive body was covered in deep gashes from the ropes, and its eyes held a mix of fear and pain.

"It's okay," Mia said softly, swimming closer. "We're here to help." The whale shuddered but stopped thrashing, its eye turning toward Mia. "It hurts," it said, its voice low and mournful.

"I know," Mia replied gently. "But we'll get you free. Just hold still, okay?" As they worked, Mia and Luke were joined by unexpected allies, a pod of Risso's dolphins. These large, gray dolphins with scarred bodies were known for their intelligence and curiosity. One of them clicked softly as it approached.

"Need help?" it asked, its round eyes filled with concern. "Yes," Mia said, smiling despite the gravity of the situation. "Can you keep the floats steady while we cut the ropes?"

The dolphins nodded, moving into position. They used their noses to nudge the buoys, keeping the ropes from tightening further as Luke sawed through the thickest lines. Mia focused on the ropes around the whale's pectoral fins, using her levitation powers to lift them gently away.

"Almost there," she said, her voice calm but determined. The work was slow and delicate, every movement calculated to avoid causing more harm. Luke cut the final rope near the tail, and Mia carefully unwound the last line from the whale's fin. When the ropes finally fell away, the young whale stretched its fins, testing its newfound freedom. It let out a deep, joyful sound that echoed through the water.

"You're free now," Mia said, her heart swelling with relief. "Thank you," the whale replied, its voice filled with gratitude. "I have to go; Hawaii is a long way away."

"Stay safe," Mia said, watching as the whale dove into the depths, its massive tail creating a wave that shimmered in the sunlight. Back on *Pitter Patter*, Mia and her dad sat on the deck, catching their breath.

The dolphins helped retrieve all the pieces of rope, traps, and floats from the water. They brought them to the back of *Pitter Patter.* Mia and her dad standing on the swim platform, collected all the old gear so it could be disposed of or reused properly. It filled the whole cockpit, but they were happy it was safely out of the ocean where it couldn't do any more harm. Mia thanked the dolphins for their help and they did several flips and jumps in reply.

"You were incredible out there," Luke said, ruffling Mia's hair. "We couldn't have done it without the dolphins," Mia replied, glancing at the pod as they swam off, their clicks and whistles echoing in the distance. As the sun dipped lower in the sky, casting a golden glow over the ocean, Luke grinned. "Still up for a dive tomorrow?"

Mia laughed. "Of course, but let's head back to the cove and cook up some dinner"

Chapter 6

The Kelp Forest Rescue

The early morning sun sparkled on the calm waters of Big Sur as *Pitter Patter* rocked gently in its anchor. Mia and her dad, were preparing to dive at Flintstones, a dive site known for its majestic underwater rock formations and thriving marine life. This spot had always been a treasure trove of kelp forests, teeming with life, and Mia was eager to explore it.

"Let's see what the ocean has for us today," Luke said as he adjusted his scuba tank.

Mia, who didn't need a tank anymore thanks to her magical ability to breathe underwater, grinned as she pulled on her fins. "I can't wait to see the kelp. It's always so full of surprises."

They slipped into the water, descending along the anchor line into what they expected to be an underwater paradise. But as they swam lower, they were met with an eerie sight.

Instead of a lush green kelp forest swaying in the current, the seafloor was covered by a barren carpet of purple sea urchins. The vibrant ecosystem they had expected was gone, replaced by an underwater wasteland. "This can't be Flintstones," Mia whispered, her voice carrying through the water.

Her dad nodded grimly, pointing to the rock formations using hand signals to indicate that it was. They swam further, their eyes scanning the rocky bottom. The kelp holdfasts, what was left of them, were gnawed down to nubs, the once-vibrant forest reduced to stumps. The spiny purple sea urchins covered every surface, their numbers so overwhelming that nothing else could thrive.

Mia felt a lump in her throat. "What happened here?" Luke took a series of photos, documenting the devastation. There wasn't anything besides the urchins to see, they ended their dive and headed to the surface.

Back aboard *Pitter Patter*, he told Mia "This is what happens when an ecosystem loses its balance. Without predators to keep the urchins in check, they multiply and eat everything in sight. The kelp doesn't stand a chance." "What can we do?" asked Mia. "I have some friends that will be really interested, we can ask them," said Luke.

As Mia and Luke headed back to Monterey Harbor, they shared their findings with scientists and conservationists at the *Giant Giant Kelp Restoration Project*. Keith, one of the project leaders, was waiting at the dock when they pulled in.

"This isn't the first barren we've seen," Keith said as he scrolled through Luke's photos. "But Flintstones used to be one of the healthiest kelp forests around. It's hard to see it like this."

"Why are there so many urchins?" Mia asked, sitting cross-legged on the dock. Keith sighed. "It's a perfect storm of problems. First, we lost most of the sunflower stars to sea star wasting disease. They were one of the main predators of urchins. Then, warmer waters caused by climate change weakened the kelp, making it easier for urchins to wipe it out. And without healthy kelp forests, otters and other predators struggle to survive. It's a domino effect."

"But isn't there anything we can do?" Mia asked.

Keith smiled faintly. "That's where the *Giant Giant Kelp Restoration Project* comes in. We've been working to remove urchins from barrens and give the kelp a chance to regrow. It's slow work, but it's effective. In areas where we've done urchin smashing, the ecosystem comes back quickly. Fish return to feed in the regrowing kelp, otters start hunting in the area again, and the balance begins to restore itself."

Mia's eyes lit up. "Can we help?" Keith grinned. "You'd need to get certified first, but we'd love to have you on the team. We always need more 'urchin smashers.'"

Over the next few weeks, Mia and her dad trained with the Giant Giant Kelp Restoration

Project team. They learned how to identify urchin species, the best techniques for removing the urchins, and the importance of leaving healthy ecosystems untouched.

"Urchin smashing isn't just about clearing the area," Keith explained during one of their dives. "It's about making room for the kelp to regrow. And when the kelp comes back, everything else does too."

Mia saw it firsthand during a training dive. They were working in an area that had been cleared of urchins just a month earlier. Tiny kelp fronds were already sprouting from the rocks, their vibrant green leaves waving in the current.

Fish darted in and out of the regrowing forest: juvenile rockfish, perch, and even a curious sheephead. The water was alive with activity, the ecosystem rapidly bouncing back. "Look at that!" Mia said, pointing to a school of fish feeding on tiny invertebrates clinging to the kelp.

Luke snapped photos, capturing the transformation. Back on the surface, they talked about their experiences under the water. "It's incredible how fast things turn around when we give them a chance." Keith nodded. "It's a powerful reminder that even small actions can make a big difference. But we need to keep the momentum going. That's why we're also working on other solutions, like restoring sunflower stars."

One afternoon, Keith invited Mia and Luke to visit the Sunflower Starfish Restoration Lab. There, researchers were breeding sunflower stars that were immune to wasting disease, hoping to reintroduce them to the wild. "These stars are incredible predators," one of the scientists explained as Mia gazed into a tank filled with juvenile stars. "They can eat dozens of urchins in a single day. If we can bring them back, they'll help keep the urchin population under control naturally."

Mia carefully picked up one of the stars, its tiny arms moving gently in her hand. She hoped that one day it would be back in the ocean helping to restore the balance.

Back on *Pitter Patter*, Mia and her dad reflected on their journey. "We've learned so much," Mia said, looking out at the ocean. "It's sad that so many ecosystems are in trouble, but it feels good to be part of the solution."

As the sun set over the bay, casting golden light on the water, Mia felt a renewed sense of purpose. The kelp forests were worth fighting for, and she was ready to do her part.

Chapter 7

Delta Dreaming

The low hum of the engine filled the air as *Pegasus*, the Kingtide family's 34-foot trawler, cut through the calm waters of the San Francisco Bay. Mia Kingtide stood on the deck, her hair whipped by the breeze, as she watched the shoreline of Northern California drift by. The trawler was heading up the Sacramento-San Joaquin Delta, a sprawling network of rivers, sloughs, and marshlands that Mia loved to explore.

"Ready to see what the Delta has in store for us?" Luke, her dad, called from the helm on the fly bridge.

"Always!" Mia replied with a grin. Trips aboard *Pegasus* gave them a change of scenery from Monterey and a chance to learn about the freshwater side of California's ecosystems.

After a few hours of cruising, they approached a narrow dock near Walnut Grove, one of the Delta's small towns. The current was stronger than expected, making it tricky to steer *Pegasus* alongside the dock.

"Mia, grab the bow line and put out that fender!" Luke instructed, focusing on the wheel as he adjusted their angle.

"I've got it," Mia said, rushing to the bow. As the boat edged closer, she grabbed the line and leaned over the side, but the gap between the boat and the dock was too wide.

"Hold on," she muttered, glancing around to make sure no one was watching. With a flick of her wrist, she used her levitation powers to lift the line and loop it smoothly around the cleat on the dock.

Luke jumped down from the helm, tying off the stern line as he noticed the perfectly secured bow line. He raised an eyebrow at Mia. "Nice throw," he said, a knowing smile tugging at his lips. Mia grinned, pretending to dust off her hands. "Just a little practice."

After securing *Pegasus*, Mia and her dad walked to a nearby fish ladder, a structure designed to help salmon and other migratory fish navigate around dams and return to their spawning grounds upstream. "This is incredible," Mia said as they leaned over the rail, watching salmon leap through the water. Each jump brought them closer to the next step of their journey.

"Salmon are some of the toughest animals out there," Luke said. "They start their lives as tiny fry in freshwater streams, then swim all the way to the ocean. When it's time to lay eggs, they travel back to the same stream where they were born."

"But how do they know where to go?" Mia asked. "It's like they have a built-in GPS," Luke replied. "They follow the scent of their home stream, even after years in the ocean."

As they walked toward a small information center near the fish ladder, Mia noticed a large tank filled with salmon fry. The tiny fish darted around, their movements quick and jerky. "They're so little," Mia said, leaning close to the glass.

"Don't worry," one of the fry said, its tiny voice carrying through the water. "We'll grow up fast." The fry swam in a loose circle, their silver scales catching the light. "You can hear us? That's cool! We're getting ready for the big journey to the ocean."

"Good luck," Mia said softly. "It's a tough trip, but you've got this."

"We'll do our best!" the fry chirped. Luke watched her with a curious expression. "Making friends with the fish?" Mia smiled. "Maybe."

Inside the information center, they explored exhibits about the Delta's role in California's water system. One display showed how rivers from the Sierra Nevada mountains flowed into the Delta, providing water for cities, farms, and wildlife.

"The Delta's like the heart of California," Luke said. "It pumps water to just about everyone in the state."

Mia studied a map showing the path of the rivers. "And it all starts with the snow in the mountains?"

"Exactly," Luke said. "That snow melts and feeds the rivers, which flow into the Delta. The water's used for farming, drinking, and keeping ecosystems alive. Without it, California wouldn't be able to grow all the food it does."

"But what about the saltwater?" Mia asked, pointing to another display about saltwater intrusion. Luke frowned. "That's a big problem. When too much freshwater is taken from the Delta, saltwater from the bay pushes farther inland. It makes the water unusable for farming and can harm the plants and animals that live here."

Mia stared at the display, her mind spinning with everything she'd learned. The Delta wasn't just a beautiful place, it was essential to the health of the entire state.

That evening, they docked at a small waterfront restaurant in Rio Vista. Mia helped secure the lines again, this time using her powers to pull a fender back into place before anyone noticed. Mia ate fresh salmon and vegetables, and Luke had fish and chips, they talked about the interconnectedness of the Delta, the rivers, and the ocean.

"That salmon probably started its life in a river just like the one we saw today," Luke said. "It's amazing to think about everything that had to happen for it to end up on our plate." Mia nodded, savoring the rich flavor. "Everything's connected, isn't it? The water, the fish, the people…" Luke raised his glass. "And it's up to us to take care of it all."

As darkness fell, *Pegasus* made its way back to their home marina in Oakley, a few miles down the river from Rio Vista. The stars reflected on the calm water, shimmering like distant waypoints on an unseen map. The air was cool and crisp, carrying the scent of the Delta, a mix of freshwater and the faintest whisper of the sea.

Mia stood at the bow, her hands resting on the rail as she gazed out over the darkened water. She felt the gentle hum of the engine beneath her feet, the steady pulse of *Pegasus* moving through the river, and she imagined where this boat might take them one day, far beyond the Delta, past the familiar coastline, to places she'd only dreamed about.

"Thanks for taking me here, Dad," she said, turning to look at him.

"Anytime," Luke said, his voice warm. "You've got the heart of a true explorer, Mia. And I think California needs more people like you."

Mia smiled, but her thoughts had already drifted further. The Delta, the rivers, the salmon fry she had spoken to, all felt connected, part of something much bigger. Someday, maybe they wouldn't just explore the waters of California. Maybe one day, they'd take *Pegasus* beyond the bay, chart a course for the wild waters of Alaska or the legendary Sea of Cortez, where whales swam beneath sapphire waves and the ocean teemed with life.

She wasn't sure when that journey would come, but she knew one thing for certain: wherever the sea called her, she would be ready.

Chapter 8

Balancing the Bully

The mural of a playful dolphin leaping over waves loomed behind Mia as she leaned against the wall during recess at the International School of Monterey. She was chatting with her best friend, Jessica, about their science project.

"We could make a food web with ocean animals," Jessica suggested, her enthusiasm bubbling. "We can show how everything is connected, like how kelp feeds fish, and otters keep urchins from eating all the kelp."

"That's perfect!" Mia replied. "We can use the pictures I took during my last dive. It'll be awesome!" But their excitement was cut short by a sharp, mocking voice.

"What's the big deal about dolphins anyway?"

They turned to see Ryan, a new boy in their grade, standing nearby with a soccer ball under his arm. His smirk was unmistakable.

"Dolphins are just stupid fish with big heads," Ryan sneered. Jessica frowned. "They're not fish. They're mammals." Ryan snorted. "Whatever, nerd."

Mia's fists were clenched. She had seen Ryan picking on other kids before, but this was the first time he had targeted Jessica directly.

"Leave her alone," Mia said, stepping between them. Ryan shrugged and walked away, tossing his soccer ball in the air as he went.

Jessica sighed. "Why is he like that?" Mia shook her head. She didn't like bullies but confronting him head-on didn't feel like the right solution. There had to be a way to stop Ryan's behavior without escalating things further.

That afternoon in science class, Ms. O'Connor introduced a new topic: ocean ecosystems and balance.

"Today, we're going to talk about food webs," Ms. O'Connor began, pointing to a diagram on the whiteboard.

"In the ocean, every animal and plant are connected. If one part of the system is removed or becomes too abundant, it can cause an imbalance."

Mia raised her hand. "Like when there are too many sea urchins, and they destroy the kelp forests?"

"Exactly," Ms. O'Connor said, smiling. "Sea urchins are natural grazers, but they need predators to keep their populations in check. Animals like sunflower stars, otters, and sheepshead fish eat urchins and keep their numbers balanced. When those predators are removed, the urchins multiply uncontrollably and eat all the kelp, creating what we call an 'urchin barren.'"

Mia sat back, thinking about the barren she and her dad had seen near Big Sur. She pictured the once-vibrant kelp forest reduced to a wasteland.

"Maintaining balance is key," Ms. O'Connor continued. "The same principle applies to other parts of life, not just the ocean."

Mia's eyes lit up. Ms. O'Connor was right balance wasn't just for ecosystems. Maybe Ryan was like the urchins, disrupting the harmony of their classroom. What he needed wasn't punishment; it was balance.

Over the next couple of days, Mia kept an eye on Ryan, trying to figure out what made him act the way he did. During lunch, she noticed he often sat alone, sketching in a notebook. Curious, she edged closer without being seen and caught a glimpse of his drawings.

The sketches were incredibly detailed pictures of soccer players in action, full of energy and movement. "He's really talented," Mia whispered to herself. But when a group of students walked by, Ryan quickly shoved his notebook into his backpack, his expression guarded.

It clicked. Ryan was afraid of being judged for what he loved, so he lashed out at others first. Mia and Jessica brainstormed a way to help Ryan feel included without making him defensive. "What if we showed him how his drawings could fit into our science project?" Jessica suggested. Mia grinned. "That's perfect! He loves soccer, right? We could show him how balance is important in a team, just like in an ecosystem."

At recess the next day, Ryan was back at it, teasing a younger student who had dropped his hat. As he tossed the hat in the air, Mia used her levitation powers to gently guide it out of his hand and back to the student.

"What the ?" Ryan muttered, looking around in confusion.

"Nice catch!" Mia said, walking up to him with a bright smile.

Ryan frowned. "What do you want, Mia?"

"I saw your drawings the other day," Mia said, ignoring his tone. "They're amazing. Have you ever thought about using them for a project?"

Ryan blinked. "What are you talking about?"

"Our science project," Mia explained. "We're making a food web, but we want to show how balance is important in other areas too, like on a soccer team. You could help us illustrate it." Ryan hesitated, his grip tightening on his soccer ball. "Why would you want my help?"

"Because you're good at drawing," Jessica chimed in, stepping up beside Mia. "And it sounds like you know a lot about soccer."

Ryan looked between them, his defensive posture softening. "I guess I could try."

Over the next week, the three of them worked together on the project. Ryan drew a vibrant diagram of a soccer team, showing how every position relied on the others to keep the game balanced. Mia and Jessica connected it to the ocean food web, explaining how kelp, urchins, and otters worked in harmony when the ecosystem was healthy.

When they presented the project to the class, even Ms. O'Connor was impressed.

"This is an excellent example of how balance applies to so many parts of life," she said. "Great job, all of you." Ryan beamed, and for the first time, Mia saw him smile without a trace of sarcasm.

At lunch that day, Mia noticed Ryan sitting with a group of kids, showing them his sketchbook. She couldn't help but smile. "You did it," Jessica said, nudging her.

"We did it," Mia corrected. "Sometimes, people just need a chance to show their best side." Jessica nodded. "Kind of like how kelp needs a little help to grow back after urchins take over." Mia grinned. "Exactly. Balance is everything."

Chapter 9

The Sunflower Star Comeback

The early morning sun cast a golden glow over Monterey Bay as Mia Kingtide stood on the deck of *Pitter Patter*, staring out at the horizon. In the distance, she could see Tanker Reef, its rocky shale formations invisible beneath the sparkling blue water but marked by the Monterey Yacht Club's yellow buoys. The reef was special to Mia, not just because it was close to home, but because it had once been one of the most vibrant kelp forests she'd ever seen.

But now, the reef was a shadow of its former self. Purple sea urchins had overrun it, turning the once lush underwater forest into a barren wasteland. The kelp had been devoured, leaving the fish and marine life that depended on it without shelter or food. The rocky substrate of the reef was now an "urchin barren," a desolate underwater expanse with little to no life.

"Ready to bring this reef back to life?" Her Dad, asked as he secured the tanks holding the young sunflower stars on the deck.

Mia nodded, her jaw set with determination. "We're going to fix this today, Dad. This reef deserves a second chance."

Luke smiled. "That's the spirit, Miss Mia. These little sunflower stars hold the key to restoring balance."

"Sunflower stars weren't just ordinary sea creatures. Growing over three feet across, with as many as 24 arms, they were one of the largest sea stars in the world. Vibrant shades of orange, purple, and yellow made them as striking as they were effective predators. Fast and agile for a sea star, they used thousands of tiny tube feet to roam the seafloor, feasting on purple sea urchins." Luke said to Mia.

"Everything was doing ok until, disaster struck in 2013 when a mysterious disease known as sea star wasting syndrome nearly wiped out the sunflower star population along the Pacific Coast. The absence of this predator had devastating consequences." Luke said. "Without sunflower stars to keep them in check, purple sea urchins multiplied unchecked, devouring nearly all of Northern California's iconic kelp forests. Almost 96% of the kelp forests have vanished, but with these Sunflower Stars, we might be able to bring some of it back"

The kelp wasn't just beautiful, Mia knew it was the foundation of an entire ecosystem. From abalone and rockfish to sea otters and leopard sharks, countless species relied on the kelp forests for food and shelter. Without kelp, the entire marine food web was at risk.

Now, thanks to pioneering projects by scientists at Moss Landing Marine Laboratories and the California Academy of Sciences, young sunflower stars were being bred in labs and reintroduced to help control the urchin population. Mia and Luke were honored to play a part in this restoration effort.

As *Pitter Patter* neared the reef, Mia and Luke prepared the tanks holding the juvenile sunflower stars in the cockpit. The young stars, about the size of dinner plates, wriggled their tube feet against the walls of their enclosures. Each star was a bright burst of color, a sign of hope for the struggling ecosystem.

"These little guys are incredible," Luke said as he carefully lifted one of the tanks. "They're voracious urchin predators. And once they grow bigger, nothing will stand in their way."

Mia donned her wetsuit, fins, and mask, securing her weight belt and green bag holding her shell around her waist. Unlike her dad, who relied on scuba gear, Mia's magical ability to breathe underwater meant she could stay below for as long as needed without the bulky equipment. She smiled as she adjusted her mask and fell backward into the water.

The cold Pacific enveloped her, and as she descended, the familiar stillness of the underwater world calmed her nerves. But the sight of Tanker Reef sent a pang through her chest. The shale reef was covered in purple sea urchins, their spiny bodies clustering over every surface. The once-flowing green kelp had been reduced to sparse, struggling strands.

Mia carefully carried a container of sunflower stars to a sheltered overhang in the reef. Gently, she released them one by one. The stars unfurled their many arms, their tube feet gripping the rocks as they began exploring their new home.

"You've got a big job ahead of you," Mia whispered, watching the stars settle in.

Luke joined her, placing another group of stars further along the reef. Together, they worked methodically, ensuring each star had plenty of space and access to the urchins they needed to feed on.

Two months later, Mia and Luke returned to Tanker Reef aboard *Pitter Patter*. As they approached the anchorage, Mia's heart raced with a mix of excitement and nervousness. Would their efforts have made a difference?

From the surface, the signs of recovery were already visible. Giant kelp fronds stretched toward the sunlight, their golden-green tips breaking the water's surface. Mia couldn't wait to dive in.

Sliding into the water, she was immediately struck by the transformation. The reef was alive again. Vibrant green kelp swayed in the current, their fronds teeming with life. Schools of fish darted through the forest, their shimmering scales catching the sunlight. Crabs scuttled across the rocks, and a graceful leopard shark glided through the dense kelp canopy.

Mia swam deeper, her chest swelling with pride. Her sunflower star friends had grown larger, their arms extending gracefully as they moved across the reef. One star was perched atop a cluster of urchins, feasting with slow, deliberate movements.

Nearby, a California sheephead fish munched on urchins as well. The sheephead, another vital predator, had returned to the reef alongside the stars. "You're doing amazing work," Mia said, smiling as she watched the reef come back to life.

Not everything was perfect. As Mia swam farther into the reef, she came across a section still dominated by urchins. The once-vibrant kelp forest had not yet returned here. The rocky shale was barren, a sea of purple spines covering nearly every surface. The kelp in this patch was sparse and struggling to regrow against the relentless grazing of the purple urchins. The scene felt stark, almost lifeless, compared to the thriving areas she had explored earlier.

"This patch needs more help," Mia said aloud, frowning as she hovered above the barren rocks.

Luna, her playful sea lion friend, noticed her pause and swam up beside her, spinning in a quick circle before darting closer. "What's wrong, Mia? Why aren't you smiling?" she asked, tilting her head as if trying to understand Mia's concern.

Mia gestured toward the barren patch. "Look at this area. The urchins are everywhere. The kelp can't catch a break. It's like the urchins are just waiting to eat whatever tries to grow."

Luna swam lower, inspecting the rocks and the urchins that crowded them. She let out an exaggerated bark of frustration. "Ugh, these little spiky guys are ruining everything! Should we bring more of those sunflower stars you released? They seemed pretty good at snacking on these pests."

Before Mia could respond, Marlow, the southern sea otter, paddled over with a crab clamped between his small paws. He floated on his back, crunching noisily, his whiskers twitching with satisfaction.

"More sunflower stars might help," he said thoughtfully between bites. "But you humans always talk about balance, don't you? Wouldn't too many predators cause new problems?"

Mia nodded, appreciating Marlow's insight. "You're right, Marlow. We can't just dump more predators in here without thinking about the long-term impact. If we add too many sunflower stars, they might eat all the urchins, but then what happens to the ecosystem when they run out of food? We need a more thoughtful approach."

Flip, the energetic harbor seal, popped his head up from below, a small cloud of disturbed sand trailing behind him. "What if we move some of the urchins away?" he suggested eagerly, his whiskers twitching.

"Like... relocate them? I don't know where they'd go, but it would be less crowded here, right?"

Mia chuckled at Flip's enthusiasm but shook her head. "It's a good idea, Flip, but purple urchins don't really belong anywhere in these numbers. If we move them, they'll just overgraze somewhere else.

We need to reduce their numbers, not just shuffle them around."

Luna twirled in the water, her sleek body cutting gracefully through the current. "Okay, so what's the plan, Captain? You're the one who talks to the humans. You figure this stuff out."

Mia sighed, glancing at the barren rocks again. "I'll talk to my dad and Keith from the Giant Giant Kelp Restoration Project. Maybe we can bring in a team to cull the urchins here by hand. It's slow work, but it could make a big difference."

Back on *Pitter Patter*, Mia explained the situation to her dad, Luke. Together, they contacted Keith from the Giant Giant Kelp Restoration Project to discuss the issue.

"You're absolutely right, Mia," Keith said over the radio. "This is a common problem in areas where urchins have overrun the reef. In cases like this, we usually cull the urchins by hand. It's slow work, but it's one of the most effective ways to give the kelp a chance to regrow."

The following week, Mia and Luke returned to Tanker Reef with a team of divers armed with hammers and collection bags. Mia's marine friends were already there, eagerly waiting to help.

"This is going to be fun!" Luna barked, her excitement evident as she zipped through the water. "We'll make sure nothing sneaks up on you while you work."

Flip grinned, his whiskers twitching with anticipation. "And if you crack open any urchins, I'll be happy to clean up the mess!"

Marlow, ever the pragmatist, floated nearby with a crab in his paws. "Just be careful, Mia. Those spiky things can be nasty if you're not paying attention."

Underwater, the divers worked carefully, using hammers to crack open the spiky purple shells of the urchins. As the insides spilled out, colorful rockfish swarmed the area, eagerly snapping up the easy meal. Flip and Luna darted through the water, keeping a watchful eye on the divers.

Marlow eventually joined the effort, expertly prying open an urchin with his teeth and claws before floating away with his prize. "Delicious!" he exclaimed, his voice muffled by the food in his mouth. "You should crack open more of these."

Mia watched her friends and the divers working together, a sense of pride swelling in her chest. "This is what teamwork looks like," she thought, her heart swelling with pride.

After hours of meticulous work, the barren patch of reef was noticeably less crowded. The divers had removed hundreds of urchins, they also brough over a few sunflower stars, to help create space for the kelp to begin its recovery.

As the sun dipped lower in the sky, Mia and her dad stood on the deck of *Pitter Patter*, watching the waves lap gently against the boat. Below them, the reef was alive with activity. Rockfish darted between the fronds of kelp, crabs scuttled across the rocks, and a sunflower star moved gracefully along the seabed, its vibrant orange arms outstretched as it feasted on the remaining urchins.

In the distance, Mia could see Luna spinning joyfully through the water while Flip playfully chased a school of fish. Marlow floated nearby, nibbling on another crab, his face serene and content.

"This is amazing," Mia said softly, her voice filled with awe. "It's not perfect yet, but it's getting there."

Luke nodded, his hand resting on her shoulder. "Restoring balance takes time, but this reef is on the right path. And with people like you and friends like Flip, Luna, and Marlow it has a bright future."

Mia smiled, gazing out at the horizon as the sun dipped into the water, casting a warm, golden glow over the bay. The challenges of restoring the ocean were vast, but so were the opportunities for change. With her magical connection to the sea and the help of her friends, human and marine alike, Mia knew they could make a difference.

Chapter 10

Cleaning Up After a King Tide

The morning sun cast a warm glow on Del Monte Beach, illuminating the chaos left behind by the recent king tide. The shoreline was buried under heaps of debris, plastic bottles, Styrofoam, fishing lines, and countless scraps of trash, all tangled with seaweed and driftwood. Mia Kingtide stood at the water's edge, her hands on her hips, surveying the scene with a heavy heart.

Mia's last name, Kingtide, felt especially significant today. Her family had always lived by the sea, and their name came from the awe-inspiring natural phenomenon of the highest tides. King tides occurred when the sun, moon, and Earth aligned, creating a gravitational pull strong enough to cause water levels to rise dramatically, often flooding coastal areas. But lately, these tides have become more extreme.

"Why are the tides getting higher, Dad?" Mia asked as her father, Luke, walked up beside her with a pair of gloves in his hands.

"Global warming," Luke explained, picking up a piece of driftwood. "Rising sea levels and melting glaciers are making king tides higher. They're washing more trash onto the shore, and it's a big problem for beaches, animals, and the ocean."

Mia frowned, watching as a plastic bag fluttered in the breeze, snagging on a clump of seaweed. "We have to clean this up. The animals can't live like this."

Luke put a hand on her shoulder. "Then let's get to work."

Mia knew this was a task too big for just her and her dad. She had rallied her classmates from the International School of Monterey earlier that week.

"Higher tides are happening more often," Mia had explained during recess. "They're bringing more trash to our beaches, and if we don't clean it up, it'll end up back in the ocean, hurting animals and polluting the water."

Her best friend, Jessica, had been the first to raise her hand. "I'm in! Dolphins are our mascot, after all. Let's protect their home!"

Soon, nearly the entire class had signed up, and even their teacher, Ms. O'Connor, had volunteered to join. By the next morning, over fifty students, parents, and community members had gathered at Del Monte Beach, armed with gloves, trash bags, and grabbers.

"This is a huge job," Jessica said as she stood beside Mia, staring at the piles of debris scattered across the sand.

Mia glanced at the waves and smiled. "We're not alone."

She waded into the shallows, letting the cool water lap at her legs. Closing her eyes, she called out "Hey, Flip, Luna and Marlow, we need your help!"

Moments later, the water stirred with movement. Flip, the energetic harbor seal, popped his head above the surface, his whiskers twitching with curiosity. "What's wrong, Mia?" he asked, splashing closer.

Luna, the playful sea lion, surfaced next, barking enthusiastically. "Are we cleaning today? I love cleaning!"

Marlow, the curious sea otter, floated nearby, nibbling on a piece of seaweed. "What's the plan this time, Mia?"

Mia explained the situation. "The king tide left a huge mess. There's trash everywhere, and we need to clean it up before it washes back into the ocean and I need your help to get the pieces that already have sunk nearby"

Flip barked excitedly. "Let's do this!"

Luna twirled in the waves. "I can push the bigger things onto the shore!"

Marlow nodded thoughtfully. "I'll focus on the tricky stuff. You know, the things tangled in seaweed."

The cleanup quickly became a coordinated effort, with the kids on land working alongside the animals in the water.

Flip dove beneath the waves, using his nimble body to nudge plastic bottles and cans toward the shore. "Here comes another one!" he called, flipping a water bottle onto the sand.

Luna, with her strong flippers, pushed larger debris, like an old boat fender and a tire, closer to Mia and Jessica. "This one's heavy, but I've got it!" she barked, her voice filled with determination.

Marlow worked meticulously, using his dexterous paws to untangle Styrofoam pieces from seaweed. "This stuff breaks into tiny pieces," he explained to Mia. "We can't let it stay in the water."

Meanwhile, the kids worked in small groups along the beach, laughing and chatting as they collected trash. Ms. O'Connor moved between groups, using the cleanup as a teaching moment.

"Did you know that 80% of the trash in the ocean starts on land?" she said, holding up a crumpled chip bag. "Every piece we pick up here makes a difference."

Jessica found a rusty crab snare tangled in a clump of seaweed. "This could've hurt a sea lion!" she exclaimed, carefully placing it in her bag.

Another classmate, Ryan, held up a piece of Styrofoam. "This stuff is the worst. It breaks into little pieces, and fish eat it, thinking it's food."

Mia smiled as she overheard the conversations. Her classmates were learning just how important this work was.

As the cleanup continued, a truck from ReGen Monterey pulled up to the beach. A woman in a bright yellow vest stepped out and waved. "You must be Mia!" she called.

"That's me!" Mia said, running over.

"I'm Tara, with ReGen Monterey. We're here to collect the trash you've gathered. We'll recycle as much as we can and properly dispose of the rest. Thanks for coordinating this effort!"

Mia beamed. "Thank you for helping! There's so much trash, and I didn't want it to all go to a landfill."

Tara nodded. "You're doing amazing work. Let's see how much of this we can turn into something useful again."

With the help of volunteers and ReGen Monterey, the bags of trash were sorted. Plastic bottles, cans, and other recyclables were separated from non-recyclable items. Even some reusable materials, like driftwood and rope, were set aside for repurposing.

By midday, the team was getting tired. Some kids slumped on the sand, overwhelmed by how much trash was still left.

"This feels impossible," Ryan muttered, dropping his grabber.

Mia climbed onto a piece of driftwood, her voice strong and encouraging. "Look how much we've already done!" she said, pointing to the growing pile of trash bags. "We've made a huge difference. And it's not just about cleaning the beach, it's about showing the ocean that we care." Jessica chimed in, "If Flip, Luna, and Marlow can keep going, so can we!"

The kids laughed; their energy renewed. They grabbed their tools and got back to work, spurred on by the playful antics of their marine helpers.

Flip leapt out of the water, tossing a piece of trash onto the shore with a triumphant splash.

"Teamwork makes the dream work!"

Luna nudged a tangle of fishing lines toward a group of kids, who cheered as they bagged it. "We're unstoppable!" she declared.

Marlow floated nearby, watching the scene unfold. "Humans and animals working together. This is how it should be."

By late afternoon, the beach was transformed. The sand was clean, the trash was bagged, and the waves sparkled under the sun. Volunteers stood proudly beside the collected debris as Tara from ReGen Monterey loaded the final bags into the truck.

"You've all done an incredible job," Tara said. "This is what community action looks like."

Mia waded into the water to thank her marine friends. "We couldn't have done it without you," she said, smiling. "You're welcome!" Luna barked, leaping out of the water. "Just make sure it stays clean," Marlow added, his tone teasing but sincere.

That evening, as Mia and her dad walked along the clean beach, Mia felt a deep sense of pride and purpose.

"Dad," she said, her voice steady. "I think I know what I want to do when I grow up."

Luke raised an eyebrow. "What's that, Mia?"

"I want to work for the Monterey Bay Aquarium Research Institute (MBARI) or Woods Hole Oceanographic Institution (WHOI). I want to design systems and submersibles to clean the ocean and teach people how to protect it. King tides are just the start we need to learn how to fix everything we're doing to the planet."

Luke smiled proudly. "That's a big goal, Mia. But

I think you're more than ready to make it happen."

"And maybe I'll write books, too," Mia added. "So kids everywhere can learn to help the ocean."

As they walked on, the horizon stretched endlessly before them, the waves lapping gently at their feet. For Mia, this was just the beginning of her journey to protect the ocean. The challenges were vast, but so were the possibilities for change.

Chapter 11

Sand Dollar Secrets

The afternoon sunbathed San Carlos Beach in warm, golden light, casting a soft glow over the sand and the gentle waves rolling onto the shore. Mia Kingtide lay stretched out on the beach, her fingers lazily sifting through the fine grains of sand as she listened to the rhythmic hush of the ocean. A few yards away, her dad was deep in conversation with the folks at Backscatter Underwater Photography, discussing new camera housing for their next dive trip.

She had tried to listen at first, but after a few minutes of words like "strobe angles" and "optical dome ports," she had let her dad know she was heading to the beach, then quietly slipped away to spend time with her real teachers, the ocean and her marine friends.

Luna, Flip, and Marlow were sprawled out nearby, enjoying the sun in their own ways. Flip lay on his belly, his flippers tucked under him as if he were pretending to be a rock. Luna had rolled onto her back, letting the warmth soak into her smooth fur. Marlow, who never left the water, was just beyond the surf line in the kelp, rubbing his paws together as he was snacking on a sea urchin.

"This," Flip sighed dramatically, closing his eyes, "is the perfect afternoon."

Mia smiled, stretching out her arms. "I have to admit, this is nice."

"Even sea creatures like a good sun nap now and then," Luna murmured, waving a flipper in the air.

Marlow lifted his head just enough to glance at Mia. "Besides, we're waiting for the tide to go out a little more. Then, you're going to see something special."

Mia propped herself up on her elbows. "Something special?"

Flip nodded, grinning. "Oh yeah. A sand dollar bed."

Mia blinked. "A sand dollar bed? Like a place where sand dollars sleep?"

Luna chuckled. "Not exactly. It's a place where thousands of them live, just under the surface of the water."

Mia had seen sand dollars before, usually as dry, white shells that were washed up on the beach, but she had never given much thought to where they lived or how they got there. Her dad always collected the ones he found after surfing, joking that he had "got paid to surf today," which never failed to make her roll her eyes. She pushed herself up to sit cross-legged in the sand.

"Alright, I'm interested. What's so special about them?"

Flip's eyes twinkled with excitement. "Oh, just that they have secret messages hidden in their patterns."

Mia gave him a skeptical look. "Secret messages?"

Marlow, ever the patient one, floated up from his spot and waded toward the water. "Come on," he said, his voice calm and knowing. "You'll understand when you see them."

She followed them down to the shallows, stepping into the cool water as the tide receded. The sand beneath her feet was smooth and soft, shifting slightly with every step. Flip swam ahead, leading her to a wide stretch of beach where the waves had pulled back just enough to reveal something extraordinary.

There, just beneath the thin layer of moving water, lay thousands of sand dollars. Some were fully exposed, their round, delicate shapes dotting the seafloor like scattered coins. Others were half-buried, barely visible beneath the shifting sand. The water around them sparkled in the sunlight, making the entire scene look like a hidden treasure trove.

Mia's mouth fell open. "Whoa. I've never seen so many in one place before."

"They like places like this," Luna said, swimming beside her. "Flat, sandy, with just the right kind of current."

Mia crouched down, her hands skimming over the wet sand as she carefully picked up a sand dollar. It was heavier than she expected, cool and smooth, with the familiar five-petal pattern on its top. She traced the ridges with her fingertip. "So where do they come from? Do they start like this?"

Marlow paddled closer, his small paws making gentle ripples in the water. "Oh no. They start out much, much smaller. Almost invisible."

Mia tilted her head. "How small are we talking?"

Flip grinned. "Tiny. Like, floating-through-the-ocean-with-the-plankton tiny." Mia's eyes widened. "Wait, sand dollars are part of the plankton?"

Luna nodded. "Yup! When they're babies, they drift through the water as larvae, along with other zooplankton. They don't look anything like this at first."

Mia studied the sand dollar in her hand, trying to imagine it as a tiny, drifting creature. "How do they grow into this?"

Marlow sat up, clearly enjoying his role as the wise one. "Well, after floating around for a few weeks, they settle on the ocean floor and begin to transform. They start growing their skeletons, which eventually form these patterns you see now."

Flip, nudging a nearby sand dollar with his nose. "When they're alive, they're covered in tiny, hair-like spines that help them move around and burrow into the sand."

Mia turned over the sand dollar in her palm, noticing the fine, velvety texture underneath. "I never thought about them actually *moving*."

"They don't move much," Marlow admitted. "But they do tilt and shift with the tide. If you hold one just right, you can feel it adjusting."

Mia placed the sand dollar flat against her hand, closing her eyes as she focused on the feeling. At first, it was still, just a solid weight in her palm. But then, she felt something, a faint vibration, like a tiny heartbeat. Then, another shift, subtle but definite.

Her eyes snapped open. "Whoa. It's moving!"

Luna grinned. "Told you."

Mia looked around at the hundreds, maybe thousands, of sand dollars scattered across the seabed, realizing for the first time that they weren't just still objects. They were alive, breathing with the ocean, responding to the water's movement in ways she had never noticed before. Each one was subtly shifting, adjusting itself in the sand, tilting just slightly with the currents.

"They can feel the ocean changing before we do," Marlow said. "They know when the tides are shifting, when the currents are changing. They move with it."

Mia traced the ridges of the sand dollar in her hand, feeling the fine texture beneath her fingers. It was strange to think that these creatures were distant relatives of starfish, yet instead of moving freely along the ocean floor with arms stretching in all directions, sand dollars spent their lives half-buried in the sand, blending in with their surroundings.

"So, if they're related to starfish, does that mean they eat the same way?" she asked, glancing up at Marlow.

"Kind of," Marlow said, shifting onto his back as he floated lazily in the shallows. "Starfish like to pry open clams and snails with their tube feet, then push their stomachs *out* of their bodies to digest them."

He wrinkled his nose. "Honestly, it's kind of gross. But sand dollars? They're way more polite about it."

Luna swam in a slow circle, her eyes glimmering with amusement. "Polite?" she repeated. "That's one way to put it."

Flip wiggled in excitement. "Sand dollars use those tiny, hair-like spines all over their bodies to move food toward their mouths. If you look underneath one, you'll see the little mouth in the center, kind of like a starfish, but smaller."

Mia turned over the sand dollar in her hand, squinting at the fine bristles on its underside. They were so tiny she hadn't noticed them before, but now she saw how they covered the entire bottom of the creature, constantly moving. "They just… sift food out of the sand?"

"Exactly!" Marlow said. "Little bits of plankton, algae, and whatever else drifts by. They move it along those tiny spines, all the way to their mouths." He paused, then added, "And they don't even need to eat every day. They can go a long time without food if they must."

Mia shook her head, amazed. "They're patient, they move with the ocean, and they can survive tough conditions."

"Yep," Flip said proudly. "Not bad for something that looks like a fancy rock, huh?"

Mia laughed, glancing back down at the sand dollar again. She had always thought of the ocean as something vast and powerful, filled with enormous creatures and dramatic forces. But now, she realized that some of its greatest mysteries were in the smallest things, the quietest things, the ones she had never thought to notice before.

"I never realized how much is happening right beneath our feet," she murmured.

Flip playfully nudged her. "That's because you humans always look up at the horizon instead of down at the details."

Mia laughed, shaking her head. "Okay, okay. I got it. The ocean has more secrets than I thought."

Luna rolled onto her back, stretching in the shallow water. "And it always will."

Mia gently placed the sand dollar back in the sand, watching as the tide roll over it, settling it into place once more.

"Thanks for the story," she whispered.

The waves washed over her hands, cool and steady, as if answering her. She sat there for a long time, just feeling the water move, watching the tiny creatures shift and breathe with the tide. The ocean had spoken to her today, not through the crash of waves or the leap of dolphins, but in the soft, silent pulse of the sand. And this time, she truly listened.

Chapter 12

Aboard the Little Mermaid

Mia Kingtide gripped the railing of *The Little Mermaid* as the boat gently rocked over the rolling swells beyond the harbor. Sunlight glinted off the water's surface, and below them, the world transformed into an underwater forest. She leaned over just enough to see past the reflection of the sky and into the depths, where golden fronds of giant kelp swayed with the currents like trees in a silent breeze. Fish darted between the long, twisting leaves, their scales flashing in the dappled light.

Jessica stood beside her, peering down into the water with wide eyes. "This is amazing," she breathed. "It's like an underwater jungle."

Mia grinned. "Exactly! This is what I get to see when I dive."

Captain Angelo, a tall, clean-shaven man with a voice as steady as the sea, stood at the helm and smiled at the excited chatter of the kids. "You all don't know how *lucky* we got today," he said, over the boat's public address system. "Normally, the water in Monterey Bay is *so* full of plankton and algae that you'd be lucky to see five feet in front of you. It's fantastic for the sea life, plankton is the foundation of the whole ocean food web, but it makes it much harder for glass-bottom boats like this, or even for scuba divers to see very far."

Jessica blinked. "Wait, so it's not always this clear?"

Mia shook her head. "Nope. Some days, it's like swimming through green pea soup."

Captain Angelo laughed. "That's a pretty good way to describe it! But today? We hit the jackpot. Over thirty-five feet of visibility! You almost *never* get a day this clear in Monterey Bay. You all picked the perfect day for a tour."

Mia's friends leaned farther over the railing, staring in awe at the crystal-clear view below. A school of opalescent anchovies darted beneath the hull, their silvery bodies flashing as they moved as one. A bat ray glided across the sandy bottom, its wide wings undulating like a bird in slow motion. Even Ryan, who usually acted too cool for everything, nodded in appreciation.

"I didn't think it'd be this… clear," he admitted. "It's way different from looking at an aquarium."

"That's because this isn't an aquarium," Mia said. "This is their home. There is so much life down there, it makes the aquarium look barren in comparison"

Captain Angelo chuckled. "That's right. What you're seeing now is a tiny piece of the wild ocean.

No glass walls, no feeding schedules, just nature doing its thing."

Out in the water, Luna, Flip, and Marlow swam alongside the boat, watching the humans with amused expressions. Flip wiggled in excitement as a group of kids pointed at him beside the boat, his sleek body twisting effortlessly in the water.

"They look like they've never seen a harbor seal before," he said, spinning in a quick circle.

"They probably haven't seen one from this close," Luna pointed out. "Besides, we're the entertainment. You should be proud."

Marlow floated calmly nearby, gnawing on a small crab he had fished up from the seafloor. As he chewed, he tapped a paw against the hull near Jessica, his dark eyes studying her intently.

Jessica gasped, pointing excitedly. "Oh my gosh, Mia, is that *Marlow*?" Mia grinned. "Yup. Looks like he's checking you out."

Marlow crunched down on the last bit of crab and smirked. "I was just wondering if she's the human who always laughs the loudest. Sounds like I was right."

Jessica giggled, covering her mouth.

"Yeah, Jessica is the one that's always laughing." Mia replied.

Jessica shook her head, smiling. "I can't believe this is your life. You get to talk to otters and seals like it's totally normal."

Mia chuckled. "I know. And I wouldn't trade it for anything."

Captain Angelo steered the boat toward the end of the breakwater, where large, dark shapes lounged across the rocks. "Alright, folks, up ahead you'll see some of Monterey's loudest and *smelliest* residents, the California sea lions," he announced with a grin.

As the boat drifted closer, the sounds of barking and bickering filled the air. Dozens of sea lions sprawled across the rocks, some dozing in the sun, others jostling for space. A few slid clumsily into the water, their bulky bodies suddenly transforming into sleek, effortless swimmers.

Jessica wrinkled her nose. "Okay, I love the ocean, but sea lions *really* stink."

Mia giggled, covering her nose. "Yeah, I was about to say something, but I didn't want to be rude."

Captain Angelo laughed. "That's just part of the package! They haul out here after long fishing trips, so that smell? That's about a hundred pounds of fish breath."

The kids groaned in mock disgust, but they kept watching, fascinated. One particularly large male sea lion let out a deep, throaty bark, shaking his thick neck as if declaring himself king of the breakwater.

"He's always doing that," Luna muttered from the water beside the boat. "The old guys always think they own the place."

Marlow, still floating just beneath the boat, smirked. "Well, to be fair… they kinda do."

Mia leaned on the railing, watching as the massive males jostled for space on the rocks, barking loudly and pushing each other with their bulky chests. She turned to Luna, who floated just off the side of the boat. "I just realized something, you're the only girl sea lion I ever see up here."

Luna smirked. "That's because I'm special." She flicked her flipper playfully before turning serious.

"But really, most of the sea lions you see here? They're the boys. My girls usually stay farther south, down in the Channel Islands and off the coast of Mexico. That's where they have their pups. The males don't stick around for that, they just fight each other up here for space, barking about who gets the best spot."

Mia glanced back at the breakwater, where the biggest males were posturing, their thick necks rippling as they bellowed challenges at each other. "That actually makes a lot of sense. So, wait… does that mean *you* left the girls behind to come up here with all these guys?"

Luna rolled her eyes. "Hey, I like to travel. And besides, someone has to keep these boys in check."

Mia laughed. "Well, that explains why I never see pups around here."

Jessica, who had been listening to her, turned to Mia. "So, how do they even *eat* if all they do is fight?"

Mia pointed toward one of the larger males, who had just slipped into the water. "They're actually *really* good hunters. Sea lions have some of the strongest bites in the animal kingdom, not because they need to tear things apart like sharks, but because they need to hold onto their food. Fish are slippery, and when they grab one, they *have* to keep hold of it. Their bite force is almost as strong as a grizzly bear's."

Ryan's eyes widened. "Wait, seriously? A *grizzly bear*?"

Mia nodded. "Yeah. And people get way closer to sea lions than they ever would to a bear."

Jessica shuddered. "I've seen people try to take selfies *right* next to them on the docks."

Luna groaned. "Yeah, and the ones that get chased, however most of the time we just head to the water if someone is bugging us."

Captain Angelo chimed in, "She's right. People don't realize how powerful sea lions are. They look cute when they're lounging in the sun, but those jaws are no joke. They can snap down with over six hundred pounds of pressure. You don't want to be on the wrong side of that bite."

Mia watched as one of the males surfaced with a fish, tossing it up in the air and catching it headfirst. He gulped it down in one motion, then let out a loud, satisfied bark. "I bet he's telling everyone that was *his* fish," she said.

Luna smirked. "Oh, he definitely is."

The boat lingered for a few more minutes before Captain Angelo turned them back toward the wharf. As they neared the dock, Mia leaned over the railing, watching the water slip past. She had wanted her friends to see the ocean the way she did, to understand its beauty, its magic. From their awed faces and endless chatter, she knew it had worked

Chapter 13

Turning Eleven, Ocean Style

The scent of garlic, simmering seafood, and fresh pasta filled the air as Mia Kingtide gazed out the large windows of *Osteria al Mare*, one of her favorite restaurants in Monterey. It was in the harbor next to Monterey Bay Boat Works where they had the work on *Pitter Patter* done. From her seat, she had a perfect view of the entire harbor, the boats gently bobbing on their mooring balls, the fishing vessels docked along wharf two unloading their catches, and further out, the breakwater where sea lions barked and lazed in the afternoon sun.

Just below the restaurant in the outer harbor, *Pitter Patter* floated peacefully on its mooring ball, waiting for its next adventure. Mia loved seeing it there, a reminder that at any moment, she and her dad could set off into the bay, just the two of them, listening to the sounds of the sea.

Her dad, Luke, sat at the head of the table, cracking open a can of sugar-free Red Bull with a sharp *hiss*. He took a sip and smirked at her. "Miss Mia, you sure know how to plan a birthday."

Mia grinned. "Of course! Pasta and seafood by the ocean, what's better than that?"

Jessica, sitting beside her, flipped open the menu and raised her eyebrow. "Wait, everything here is local?"

Mia nodded excitedly. "Yep! The squid and halibut are caught right here in the bay, the beef and chickens come from the Salinas valley and the pasta is handmade. That's why it's so good."

Just then, a familiar voice greeted them.

"Ah, *Miss Mia!* Happy birthday, *cara mia!*"

Mia's face lit up as Maurizio, the owner of *Osteria al Mare*, approached their table. His warm Italian accent was as familiar as the ocean breeze that drifted through the open windows. Maurizio had owned the restaurant for years, and he knew Mia and her dad well, after all, *Pitter Patter* was moored right outside his restaurant.

"Maurizio!" Mia beamed. "Thanks for saving us the best table."

"Of course, of course!" he said, clasping his hands together. "For my favorite ocean explorer, only the best. Today, you celebrate eleven years, very important! And we celebrate with the best food from *our* beautiful Monterey Bay." He tapped his notepad. "So, what will it be today?"

Mia didn't hesitate. "I'll have the spaghetti ai frutti di mare, the seafood pasta with fish and calamari."

Jessica nudged her. "You know what? That sounds amazing. I'll have the same."

Ryan leaned back in his chair, still scanning the menu. "Alright, I'll go for the halibut piccata, is it local?"

Maurizio put a hand over his heart. "*Ma certo!* Of course! The halibut was landed this morning from just outside the harbor, and the squid comes fresh from the bay."

Mia beamed. "See? That's why this place is the best."

As Maurizio finished jotting down their orders, he lingered at the table with a knowing smile. "Ah, *Miss Mia*, you always ask for the best from the bay."

Mia perked up, resting her elbows on the table. "I know they catch squid at night using lights, right? But what else makes the Monterey squid fishery so special?"

Maurizio put a hand over his heart, nodding in approval. "*Ma certo!* You are correct! The fishermen use purse seiners, but unlike some other fisheries, the market squid fishery here in Monterey is very well managed. The state limits the total catch each season, and the boats can only fish on certain days to protect the squid population."

Luke leaned back in his chair, taking a sip of his sugar-free Red Bull. "It's one of the best examples of sustainable fishing. They only take squid when they're fully mature and spawning, which means they've already had a chance to reproduce before being caught. When the squid is spawning it also make for an amazing night dive."

Maurizio nodded. "Yes, exactly! The boats, purse seiners, use large nets, but they are very careful.

Most of what they catch is squid, and there is very little bycatch, unlike some other fisheries that end up catching turtles, sharks, or fish that aren't meant to be in the nets."

Mia grinned. "So, they're fishing responsibly, taking just the right amount while making sure other animals don't get caught?"

"*Perfetto!*" Maurizio beamed. "And because squid grow so fast and reproduce quickly, they can bounce back easily as long as we don't take too much. That's why squid from Monterey Bay is some of the best seafood you can eat."

Jessica, listening in, raised an eyebrow. "Wait, so that means if I order calamari at some random place, it might not be from here?"

Mia nodded. "Exactly. A lot of squid in the U.S. actually comes from China or other places where they don't have as many rules. But here, they make sure to keep the ocean balanced."

Ryan, who had been listening while scrolling on his phone, looked up. "So, I guess we're eating some of the best seafood, huh?"

Maurizio grinned. "*Sempre!* Always! That is why I am proud to serve it." He patted the table and stood up. "Alright, I go make sure your pasta is *perfetto!*"

Mia leaned back in her chair, feeling even better about her choice. The more she learned about how the ocean worked, the more she appreciated places like *Osteria al Mare* that did things the right way.

Maurizio gave Mia a knowing smile. "And let me guess, you'll want a scoop of our house-made gelato for dessert?"

Mia's face lit up. "Obviously. Stracciatella,

please."

He winked. "*Perfetto!* Be right back with your drinks."

Mia sighed happily and leaned back in her chair. She loved everything about today, the ocean, the food, her friends, and most of all, the fact that she was finally eleven.

As they waited for their food, Mia's eyes caught the familiar Seafood Watch Approved logo at the bottom of the menu.

Jessica followed her gaze. "Hey, isn't that the Monterey Bay Aquarium program? You talk about it all the time."

Mia nodded excitedly. "Yeah! It helps people choose seafood that's caught or farmed in ways that don't hurt the ocean. Some fishing methods catch too many other animals by accident, like sea turtles, sharks, and dolphins, and some fish are taken out of the ocean faster than they can reproduce. But if a restaurant or market follows Seafood Watch recommendations, it means they're getting their seafood from sustainable sources."

Ryan, who had just taken a sip of his soda, raised an eyebrow. "So, if a place doesn't have that symbol, does that mean the fish is bad?"

"Not *bad*," Mia said, "but maybe not the best choice for the ocean. Some fish are overfished, meaning they're being caught faster than they can reproduce. Seafood Watch helps people figure out what's okay to eat and what should be left alone to recover."

Jessica pulled out her phone. "Oh! They have an app. You can check before you order."

Mia nodded. "Exactly! And after lunch, we're

going to the Monterey Bay Aquarium so you guys can see more about it. It's one of my favorite places."

Luke smirked. "I knew you'd find a way to turn your birthday into an ocean field trip."

Mia shrugged playfully. "What can I say? It's the best way to spend the day."

Just as their food arrived, Maurizio surprised them by clapping his hands. "Alright, everyone, let's hear it for Mia, she's officially ELEVEN today!"

The entire restaurant, from nearby diners to the kitchen staff, clapped and cheered. Mia's face turned red, but she couldn't stop smiling.

As the steaming plates of pasta and seafood were placed in front of them, the birthday excitement continued. After they had eaten, it was time for gifts.

Mia carefully unwrapped the first package, her heart swelling with excitement.

Jessica handed her a new dive logbook, its pages blank and waiting to be filled with underwater adventures.

Ryan slid a wrapped package toward her. "This one's from me. And don't worry, no plastic."

Mia unwrapped it and gasped. It was a waterproof marine life identification guide, perfect for identifying creatures she encountered on dives.

Another friend grinned as she passed over her gift. "I figured you'd like this."

Mia opened it to find a set of reusable bamboo utensils in a fabric case. "Since you always say plastic is the worst, I thought this would be good for trips and school." Mia beamed. "This is *awesome!*"

One by one, she unwrapped more gifts, a beautifully illustrated book on ocean conservation, a pair of new dive gloves, and a handmade bracelet woven from recycled fishing nets. There was one last gift to open,

But the best part? Not a single gift had been wrapped in plastic. Instead, there were fabric bags, recyclable paper, and even one gift tied up in seaweed-dyed cloth.

Mia looked around at her friends, her chest warm with gratitude. "Thank you, guys. Seriously. You all *get* me. No plastic, no waste… just things that help me do what I love. This means a lot."

There was one last gift to open. A small, neatly wrapped package sat in front of Mia, tucked inside a soft fabric case black with blue trim and zippers. Her dad, Luke, gave her a knowing smile as she carefully untied the ribbon, her fingers trembling slightly with anticipation.

Inside, nestled inside, was a Shearwater Teric dive computer watch, sleek and powerful, with a teal face and a black strap. The moment she saw it, Mia's breath hitched. She had seen dive computers before, had even borrowed her dad's Shearwater Perdix a few times, but this? This was hers.

Her fingers traced the smooth edges of the watch, its screen reflecting the restaurant's warm lights. It wasn't just any dive computer, it was one of the best. With this, she would always know her depth, her bottom time, and how long she could safely stay underwater. Whether even though she could breath underwater thanks to the shell, they didn't know her limits, now she would never have to second-guess herself on staying safe.

She turned to her dad, her eyes wide. "Really?" she whispered. Luke nodded, his expression soft.

"Really, Miss Mia. You're ready for it. And now, no matter where you are, you'll always be able to look at your wrist and know where you are going in the ocean."

Mia swallowed hard, emotions bubbling up in her chest. This wasn't just a dive computer. It was a promise, that the ocean would always be there for her, that her dad believed in her, and that she was growing into the kind of diver who could carry this responsibility. She would only take it off to charge it when she sleeps.

Slipping it onto her wrist, she gave the strap a gentle tug to secure it. It fit perfectly, like it was always meant to be there. She tapped the buttons on the sides, cycling through its features, depth, dive time, compass, all the information she would ever need on land and beneath the waves.

She looked up at her dad and grinned. "I love it. Thank you." Luke ruffled her hair. "Figured you might."

As the plates were cleared, Maurizio returned with a bowl of house-made gelato, a single candle flickering on top. "Make a wish, birthday girl," he said with a smile.

Mia closed her eyes, breathing in the perfect moment, the ocean outside, *Pitter Patter* bobbing in the bay, her friends surrounding her, and the excitement of what was still to come.

She made her wish and blew out the candle. "Alright!" Luke said, clapping his hands together. "Who's ready for the aquarium?" The table erupted in cheers. Mia jumped up, practically bouncing with excitement.

As they left the restaurant, she took one last

look at the bay, the waves rolling in under the bright afternoon sun. This had already been the best birthday ever, and the day wasn't even over yet.

She had a feeling the next stop was going to be even more magical.

Chapter 14

Voices of the Aquarium

Mia Kingtide practically bounced on her feet as she led her friends toward the entrance of the Monterey Bay Aquarium, her excitement bubbling over like an incoming tide. She had been here countless times, but today felt different, it wasn't just any visit. Today, she was bringing her best friends into her world, the place where the ocean spoke to her even when she wasn't in the water.

The aquarium's sleek, ocean-inspired architecture stretched along Cannery Row, its massive windows reflecting the deep blues and shimmering silvers of the bay behind it. Waves lapped against the rocky shoreline just beyond the deck, where cormorants perched on sun-warmed stones, drying their wings. The salty scent of the ocean mixed with the aroma of kelp and distant fish markets, filling the air with something distinctly Monterey.

Mia's heart pounded with anticipation. Inside these walls, some of her oldest ocean friends were waiting. The animals here weren't just exhibits, they were part of her life, creatures she had known for years, each with their own story to tell.

Jessica, Ryan, and the others followed behind her, looking up in awe as they approached the entrance.

"Wow," Jessica breathed. "It's huge."

Ryan, who had been to plenty of aquariums but never this one, nodded. "I knew this place was famous, but… it's something else seeing it in person."

Luke, standing just behind Mia, smiled as he took in the view. The Monterey Bay Aquarium wasn't just special to Mia, it had changed his life too.

"You know," Luke said, glancing at the towering glass facade, "this place and the scuba diving is the whole reason I moved to Monterey."

Mia turned toward her dad, already knowing the story but loving to hear it again. "I was just about to tell them!" she said with a grin.

Luke chuckled. "Well, when I was a kid growing up in Canada, I used to watch every documentary I could about the ocean with my dad who had been scuba diving since the 70s, and so many of them talked about the Monterey Bay Aquarium. It was one of the first places that really focused on conservation, on protecting the ocean, not just putting animals in tanks. They were the first ones to figure out how to keep a great white shark in an exhibit and study it safely before releasing it. They helped restore the sea otter population. They proved that you can show people the beauty of the ocean without harming it."

Jessica's eyes widened. "So, you moved here just because of the aquarium?"

Luke nodded. "Pretty much. I knew I had to live by the ocean, and Monterey Bay felt like the right place. Now, we can see the aquarium right from the living room window of our house across the bay."

Mia smiled. She had grown up with the aquarium practically in her backyard. It had shaped who she was, just like it had shaped her dad before her.

Then Luke added, "And I was actually one of the lucky ones who got to see the great white shark they had on display."

Mia's friends' jaws practically dropped.

"Wait, you saw it?" Ryan asked.

Luke nodded. "Not many people did. It wasn't here for long, but it was incredible. Seeing a real white shark up close, watching it move through the water, it was something I'll never forget. The aquarium only kept it for a short time before releasing it back into the wild, but that was the whole point. It was never about keeping sharks forever; it was about learning and showing people that these animals aren't monsters, they're just misunderstood predators."

Mia looked at her dad with admiration. She had heard the story before, but it always gave her chills.

Luke clapped his hands together. "Alright, Miss Mia, where to first?"

Mia grinned, her eyes shining like sunlight on water. "The Giant Pacific Octopus, obviously."

They made their way through the Oceans Edge passing the kelp forest tank, before reaching the dimly lit habitat of the Giant Pacific Octopus. Soft blue lighting filtered through the exhibit, mimicking the shadowy depths where these intelligent creatures liked to hide.

The octopus sat curled inside its den, its deep-red skin shifting subtly in color as it observed the visitors pressing up against the glass. Though many people admired these creatures, few truly understood them. But Mia did.

The octopus unfurled one long arm, its suckers pressing gently against the glass as it shifted toward her. Its deep-maroon color brightened into a swirling mix of pink and silver, a playful display of recognition.

Mia smiled, placing her hand against the barrier in return.

"You're back," the octopus murmured, its voice younger and more energetic than the older octopus Mia had once known here.

Mia grinned. "Of course! I couldn't celebrate my birthday without visiting you."

Jessica, Ryan, and the others exchanged bewildered glances.

"Wait… the octopus knows you?" Jessica asked, eyes wide.

Mia turned to them, still beaming. "We just

met a few weeks ago when he was first big enough to go on public display." She glanced back at the cephalopod. "How are you liking your new home?"

The octopus rippled amber, its suckers flexing along the glass. "It's different, but I like it. The water is always clean, and there's plenty to explore. Plus, I get to meet so many humans every day."

Mia nodded, then turned to her friends. "He says it's different, but he likes it! He has plenty of space and gets to meet a lot of new people."

Ava tilted her head. "Wait… so he actually likes meeting people?"

Mia listened as the octopus flashed a soft blue, a sign of amusement. "Most of them, yes. But I don't like the bright flashes."

Mia frowned. "Oh, the camera flashes?"

The octopus wrinkled its skin slightly, almost like a frown. "Yes. Too sudden. Too bright. I like seeing the faces of the visitors, but not the flashing lights."

Mia sighed. "He says he likes meeting people, but the camera flashes are too bright. It surprises him, and he doesn't like it."

Ryan scoffed. "Yeah, that makes sense. Imagine someone constantly flashing a flashlight in your face."

The octopus coiled an arm into a spiral, watching a young child press his hands against the glass nearby. Its color deepened into a rich, shadowy brown as it sank back into its den, then, in an instant, it flashed a brilliant white, startling the child into giggles.

Jessica gasped. "Did he just, did he just prank that kid?"

Mia laughed as the octopus shimmered pink and

gold, clearly pleased with itself. "Oh yeah. They're *really* good at that."

The octopus wiggled the tip of one tentacle. "It's fun," it admitted. "They press their faces against the glass, and I disappear. Then I change color when they least expect it."

Mia grinned. "He says he loves playing tricks on the younger kids."

Ryan chuckled. "I respect that. Ultimate hide-and-seek champion."

The octopus waved a single arm, as if acknowledging the compliment. "But I also like the ones who just… watch." Its eyes turned to Mia, studying her. "Like you."

Mia's chest warmed. "I could watch you all day."

The octopus shifted into a swirling blend of deep maroon and silver, its version of a smile. "The humans stare and wonder but they don't realize I am watching them as well."

The octopus curled one arm into a spiral, pressing its suckers gently to the glass one last time.

Mia turned to her friends. "He says he's happy here because he can teach people. And that I'll help them understand why his species is so special."

Jessica smiled softly. "I think I get it."

Mia knew she did. That was the whole point.

Next, they wandered into the Sea Otter Exhibit, one of the most popular parts of the Monterey Bay Aquarium. The enclosure was a lively world of swirling water, floating kelp, and the constant movement of sleek-furred otters. Some wrestled playfully, tumbling in somersaults beneath the surface, while others floated on their backs, cracking open shellfish or grooming their dense fur, the thickest of any mammal on Earth.

The aquarium had been rescuing and rehabilitating injured and orphaned sea otters for years, and many of the otters here had once been wild. Some, like Rosa, stayed because they liked humans too much after their release and needed to come back. Even though she failed out in the ocean on her own she still had an important role to play.

The moment Mia stepped up to the glass, Rosa, one of the larger otters, perked up. She had a distinct white muzzle, a sign of her age, but her eyes were sharp and full of wisdom. She paddled over quickly, pressing her small black paws against the glass in excitement.

"Marlow's girl!" she called, her whiskers twitching. "How is he? Is he eating well? Staying out of trouble?"

Mia giggled. "Hi, Rosa! He's fine. He's being… well, Marlow."

Rosa sighed dramatically and rolled onto her back. "That boy. Always so independent. But as long as he's healthy and happy, I won't worry too much."

Ryan stared at Mia, then at the otter, then back at Mia. "Wait, wait, wait. This otter is… Marlow's mom?"

Mia shook her head. "Not his real mom. But she was his surrogate mom when he was little. The aquarium has a whole program where they pair orphaned sea otter pups with adults who teach them how to be otters. Rosa helped raise him when he was rescued as a baby."

Jessica's eyes widened. "Wait, so she was a foster mom for otters?"

Mia nodded enthusiastically. "Exactly! The aquarium rescues orphaned pups and pairs them with experienced female otters, like Rosa. She and the others teach them how to dive, hunt, and groom their fur, all the survival skills they need to go back into the wild. That way, when they're released, they don't think of humans as their parents."

Ryan crossed his arms. "That's actually… really cool."

Jessica leaned in closer to the glass. "So, Rosa helped raise Marlow, and then they released him back into the wild?"

Mia nodded her head. "Yes, he was different from the start. He always did things his own way, and when it was time for him to be released, he stayed in the bay near the aquarium. He helped me clear the aquarium intake pipes a few months ago from an old life raft and now just likes hanging out with me."

Mia pressed her hand to the glass, warmth spreading through her chest. "Thanks, Rosa."

The otter rolled onto her back, kicking up a playful splash of water. "Tell him I am thinking about him! And remind him to groom his fur properly, I know how lazy he can be."

Mia laughed. "I will!"

Rosa gave her one last affectionate glance before flipping backward, disappearing into the swaying kelp where the other otters were batting a ball around.

Mia watched, feeling a deep sense of respect for Rosa and the other otters. Even though they could never return to the ocean, they were still helping to protect it, one orphaned pup at a time.

They followed the winding pathways into the Open Sea Exhibit, where the air grew cooler, and the lighting dimmed to mimic the vast, blue world beyond the glass. Then, suddenly just past some of the amazing jellyfish exhibits, the million-gallon tank stretched in front of them, a massive window that looked as if it was opening into the open ocean itself.

It was mesmerizing. Schools of shimmering sardines pulsed through the water in perfect synchronization, forming and reforming like living silver ribbons. Giant yellowfin tuna glided effortlessly past the glass, their powerful bodies slicing through the currents. Above them, hammerhead sharks moved with eerie grace, their wide, scanning heads turning slightly as they passed.

And in the middle of it all, drifting gently on the slow-moving current, was Titan, a green sea turtle, his shell weathered with age, his wise, wrinkled face full of quiet understanding.

Mia barely had to move before Titan turned toward her. His ancient eyes locked onto hers as he glided closer, his large flippers moving in slow, steady strokes.

"It's been a while, little swimmer," Titan rumbled, his deep voice vibrating through the water.

Mia smiled warmly. "Hi, Titan."

Jessica gasped, her hands pressing against the glass. "You know the sea turtle too?!"

Mia nodded. "Titan's been here a long time. He was rescued when he was little, and he can't go back to the wild."

Titan blinked slowly; his heavy-lidded eyes filled with wisdom.

Mia explains to Jessica. "He teaches people what's worth protecting."

Titan drifted closer, his leathery flippers stretching wide as he turned slightly, revealing the unique patchwork of scars along his shell.

"The waters here… they are not like the ones I once knew," he mused, watching a school of sardines flicker past him like a living current. "The fish never leave, the tides never change, and the moon does not call the waves."

Mia tilted her head. "You miss the ocean?"

Titan blinked slowly. "At times. But this place… it is strange and beautiful in its own way. There is always food, always calm waters. The sharks here swim in circles, never hunting. The currents do not pull me far from where I rest."

He turned slightly, watching as a hammerhead glide lazily past, its body twisting smoothly with every beat of its powerful tail.

"I once feared these creatures," Titan admitted. "In the wild, they are swift, relentless. But here? They pass me by, and we are old friends. No hunger drives them. No chase ever begins."

Mia watched the hammerheads in a new light, realizing that even apex predators behaved differently here. "They get fed, so they don't need to hunt."

Titan gave a slow, thoughtful nod. "Strange, isn't it? The ocean teaches us that everything moves, hunts, flees, survives. And yet, here, the rules do not apply."

Mia frowned, watching the massive sharks loop through the water. "That's… kinda weird to think about."

Titan hummed in agreement. "It is… a different kind of life. Not better, not worse. Just different." His eyes found Mia again. "Perhaps that is the lesson. Even in still waters, one may find purpose."

Mia felt a weight settle in her chest, not a sad one, but a meaningful one.

Titan had no tides to follow, no great migrations across the sea, yet he still had a role. He had become an ambassador, teaching people about creatures they might otherwise never see in the wild.

She smiled. "You do have a purpose, Titan. A really important one."

Titan rumbled a low chuckle. "And so do you, little swimmer."

Mia pressed her palm against the glass. "Thank you."

Titan dipped his head before turning and drifting once more into the blue at the back of the exhibit.

Finally, they reached the Kelp Forest Exhibit, Mia's favorite place in the entire aquarium. The moment she stepped inside, she felt her entire body relax, as if the very presence of the towering golden kelp could settle her thoughts.

The massive, three story floor-to-ceiling tank stretched before them, its underwater forest dancing with the rhythm of the currents. Sunlight streamed down through the water in golden beams, illuminating the giant kelp fronds as they swayed, their long stalks reaching toward the surface. Rockfish hovered in the shadows, their spotted bodies blending seamlessly with the shifting light. Bright orange garibaldi darted between the kelp, their scales flashing like tiny suns. A leopard shark glided lazily through the water, weaving between the tall stalks, its sleek body barely making a ripple.

Mia pressed her hands against the railing in front of the glass, feeling a familiar sense of peace wash over her. Even from behind the glass, the kelp forest felt alive, a breathing, moving world full of hidden wonders.

"This is it," she whispered. "This is why I care so much."

Her friends stood beside her, silently watching the mesmerizing sway of the kelp. The forest pulsed with life, a world within a world, both delicate and powerful, fragile yet resilient.

"It's beautiful," Jessica murmured.

Mia nodded. "This place, this whole ecosystem, it's why we have to protect the ocean. It's not just about fish or sharks or squid. It's about the whole balance of life."

A voice behind them chuckled, warm and knowing.

"That's a smart way to look at it."

Mia turned, and her eyes widened. Standing there was Dr. Steven Webster, one of the founders of the aquarium.

Luke grinned. "Well, if it isn't the man who helped start all of this."

Dr. Webster smiled warmly. He was an older man now, with kind eyes that had seen the ocean transform over the decades. But despite the years, his passion for the sea remained as strong as the tides.

"And if it isn't young Mia Kingtide," he said, eyes twinkling. "I've heard about you."

Mia's mouth fell open. "You, you know who I am?"

He chuckled. "Word travels fast in a place like this. You've been inspiring a lot of people."

Mia felt a warmth bloom in her chest, a mixture of surprise, pride, and deep responsibility. "I just want to help."

Dr. Webster nodded. "Then you're already on the right path."

Jessica leaned in toward Mia and whispered, "Wait... *who is this guy?*"

Mia turned back, practically bubbling with excitement. "Dr. Webster is one of the founders of the aquarium! Back in the late 1970s, he and a group of scientists and ocean lovers decided that instead of taking from the sea, Monterey should be a place where people could come to learn from it."

Luke nodded. "Back then, people still thought of Monterey mostly as a fishing town. Cannery Row was built on sardines, and when the fish disappeared, the town almost collapsed with it. But instead of letting Monterey fade into history, Dr. Webster, Nancy Burnett and her husband Robin, and Chuck Baxter turned it into something new. Nancy was the daughter of David Packard, one of the founders of the computer company Hewlett-Packard and her sister Julie Packard, was the executive director of the Aquarium for 40 years, they put Monterey on the map."

Dr. Webster chuckled. "That's right. We wanted to create a place that showed the ocean as it really is, alive, and ever-changing. We didn't want it to be a typical aquarium full of small tanks and tropical fish. We wanted people to step inside an ecosystem, to see the kelp forests, the deep sea, the open ocean, and to understand how all of it is connected."

Mia turned back to the massive kelp exhibit, her heart swelling with admiration. "And now people come from all over the world just to see this."

Dr. Webster nodded. "More than two million visitors a year. And you know what? Some of them walk away forever changed, just like your dad did."

Luke smiled. "He's right. If it weren't for this place, I never would have moved to Monterey Bay."

Dr. Webster's eyes twinkled. "And if I'm not mistaken, Mia, I'd say the ocean has big plans for you too."

Mia turned back to the kelp forest, the towering golden fronds swaying like underwater trees, their blades catching the filtered light that danced through the water. She watched as the leopard shark weaved between the stalks, as the rockfish hovered in quiet patience, as the bright orange garibaldi flitted through the shadows like a flicker of fire beneath the waves.

Her heart pounded with excitement, but it was more than that, it was a calling.

She had always known she was meant to be part of the ocean. She had felt it in the pull of the tides, in the whisper of the waves, in the way the salt air wrapped around her like an old friend. But now, standing here, surrounded by the people and creatures who shared her love for it, she felt something more.

Her gift, her ability to understand and speak with the creatures of the sea, the way she can stay under the water without scuba gear and how if she puts her mind to it, she can move things, wasn't just what she had been born with. It was something the octopus and the ocean had given her.

A gift of connection, of understanding, of responsibility.

She had always thought of her powers as a secret, a wonder she was lucky to have. But it was more than that. It was a way to protect the ocean. To be its voice when it couldn't speak for itself.

She could listen to the animals, understand their struggles, learn from them in a way no one else could. She could tell their stories, help people see the ocean through their eyes. And maybe, just maybe, that would change things.

She pressed her hand against the glass, feeling the coolness seep into her palm, imagining that instead of a barrier, it was an invitation.

She wasn't just part of it.

She was one of its guardians.

She was going to protect it.

You Can Be an Ocean Hero!

Just like Mia Kingtide, you have the power to help the ocean! Every little action counts—whether it's picking up trash on the beach, using less plastic, or learning about the amazing animals that call the ocean home. By protecting the ocean, you're helping sea turtles, dolphins, whales, and even tiny plankton that make the world a better place for everyone. Remember, when we take care of the ocean, it takes care of us. So, grab your friends and family, and let's work together to keep our seas sparkling clean and full of life!

Partnering with or supporting these organizations can help amplify your efforts to protect marine ecosystems.

USA-Based Organizations

Monterey Bay Aquarium Research Institute (MBARI)
Marine research, ocean technology, and conservation.
Get Involved: Education programs, internships, volunteer opportunities.
www.mbari.org

MBARI has a fantastic Open House in July that should not be missed!

Giant Giant Kelp Restoration Project (G2KR)
Dedicated to protecting and actively restoring California's kelp forest
Get Involved: Urchin Culling, educational programs, grassroots activism.
g2kr.com

The Sunflower Star Laboratory
Researching and developing sustainable conservation aquaculture methods for sunflower star conservation and reintroduction.
Get Involved: Donate or Volunteer to help new Sunflower Stars return to the bay.
sunflowerstarlab.org

Ocean Conservancy
Fighting for trash-free seas, protecting Arctic and coastal ecosystems.
Get Involved: International Coastal Cleanup, policy advocacy, donations.
www.oceanconservancy.org

Surfrider Foundation
Clean beaches, ocean protection, and climate action.
Get Involved: Beach cleanups, grassroots activism, membership.
www.surfrider.org

NOAA Marine Debris Program
Reducing marine debris through research, removal, and prevention.
Get Involved: Educational resources, cleanup initiatives, grants.
marinedebris.noaa.gov

Pacific Marine Mammal Center
Rescuing and rehabilitating marine mammals in California.
Get Involved: Donations, internships, volunteer opportunities.
www.pacificmmc.org

Marine Conservation Institute
Protecting marine ecosystems through research and advocacy.
Get Involved: Support marine protected areas (MPAs), advocacy campaigns.
marine-conservation.org

Global Organizations

The Ocean Cleanup
Removing plastic pollution from the ocean and preventing riverborne trash.
Get Involved: Donations, educational resources, technology development.
www.theoceancleanup.com

Plastic Oceans International
Addressing plastic pollution through education, science, and advocacy.
Get Involved: Educational campaigns, events, donations.
plasticoceans.org

World Wildlife Fund (WWF) – Oceans Program
Conserving marine species, protecting ecosystems, and reducing threats to oceans.
Get Involved: Advocacy, educational programs, donations.
www.worldwildlife.org

Mission Blue
Creating and protecting "Hope Spots"—areas critical to the health of the ocean.
Get Involved: Hope Spot nominations, advocacy, support.
mission-blue.org

PADI AWARE Foundation
Marine conservation through diving education and citizen science.
Get Involved: Dive Against Debris programs, marine species protection.
www.padi.com/aware

International Union for Conservation of Nature (IUCN) – Marine and Polar Programme
Supporting global efforts to protect marine biodiversity.
Get Involved: Policy development, conservation projects, scientific studies.
www.iucn.org

UN Environment Programme (UNEP) – Clean Seas Campaign
Reducing marine litter and plastic pollution globally.
Get Involved: Advocacy campaigns, partnerships, educational initiatives.
www.cleanseas.org

Ocean Wise
Promoting sustainable seafood, reducing ocean pollution, and marine research.
Get Involved: Education programs, research, sustainable seafood initiatives.
ocean.org

Academic and Research Institutions

Woods Hole Oceanographic Institution (WHOI)
Ocean science and engineering.
www.whoi.edu

Scripps Institution of Oceanography (USA)
Marine biology, climate science, and oceanography.
scripps.ucsd.edu

Oceanographic Museum of Monaco
Marine research and public education.
www.oceano.org

Schmidt Ocean Institute
Advancing oceanographic research through technology and exploration.
schmidtocean.org

How to Get Involved

Volunteer: Join local beach cleanups, citizen science projects, or educational programs.

Advocate: Support policies that protect marine environments.

Donate: Contribute to organizations focused on ocean conservation.

Educate: Share resources and knowledge about ocean conservation with your community.

Collaborate: Partner with schools, nonprofits, and research institutions to raise awareness and fund projects.

Each of these organizations plays a unique role in safeguarding our oceans, and your participation can make a big difference!

Pitter Patter
26ft Shamrock 260 Express

PEGASUS
CHB AFT CABIN TRAWLER

Mia Kingtide : Guardian of the Coast is Availible now! Read the first chapter!

Chapter 1

A Cry for Help

The morning sun shimmered on the gentle waves as Mia Kingtide and her dad, Luke, paddled their tandem green kayak toward the sandy shore of Año Nuevo State Park. Behind them, Pitter Patter, their 26-foot cruiser, bobbed lightly on its anchor in a sheltered cove. The rugged coastline stretched out before them, dotted with windswept dunes and rocky outcroppings.

Mia leaned forward in her seat at the front of the kayak, gripping her paddle tightly. "This place is so beautiful," she said, her voice full of wonder. Luke, seated behind her, smiled as he steered them toward the shore. "It's one of my favorite spots," he said.

"And I'll bet the elephant seals will be even more incredible up close."

The tandem kayak glided smoothly through the water, the bright green hull contrasting against the deep blue waves. As they neared the beach, Mia could already hear the distant grunts and barks of the seals. It was a sound that carried a mix of power and mystery, drawing her curiosity even more.

Twelve-year-old Mia had always loved the ocean it was impossible not to, growing up on the shores of Monterey Bay. Her life changed two years ago when she rescued an octopus being harassed by older kids while trapped in a tide pool. After Mia freed it, the octopus returned with an extraordinary gift: a magical shell.

The shell transformed Mia's connection to the ocean. It gave her the ability to communicate with most marine creatures, breathe underwater without scuba gear, and even move objects without touching them in certain situations. While she was still discovering the full extent of her powers and their meaning, one thing was clear: Mia was determined to use her gifts to protect the oceans and the creatures that call them home.

After pulling the kayak onto the sand and securing it with a rope tied to a log of driftwood, Mia and Luke began their walk toward the observation areas. The air was filled with the cries of seabirds and the rhythmic crashing of waves, creating the perfect soundtrack for their adventure.

As they followed the marked path through the dunes, Mia's eyes widened at the sight of the seals basking on the beach. The massive males, with their distinctive trunk-like noses, lay sprawled across the sand, while smaller females and juveniles rested nearby.

"Look at them," Mia whispered, her excitement bubbling over.

"They're amazing, aren't they?" Luke said, pulling out his camera to take a few photos.

But as they walked farther along the path, a faint, high-pitched cry reached Mia's ears. She stopped in her tracks, tilting her head to listen.

"Dad," she said, her brow furrowing. "Do you hear that?"

Luke paused, lowering his camera. "I hear it. Sounds like a pup… over there down that gully by the driftwood."

Mia quickened her pace, following the sound until she spotted the source—a small elephant seal pup huddled behind a large log of driftwood. Its gray, mottled skin was streaked with sand, and its dark, watery eyes were wide with fear.

The pup let out another faint cry, struggling weakly to move but collapsing back onto the sand.

"Oh no," Mia murmured, kneeling a few feet away. She could feel the pup's fear radiating like a wave.

"Hey there," she said softly, reaching out with her powers to communicate. "What's wrong?"

The pup's cries quieted as it turned its gaze toward her. "You… you can hear me?" it asked, its voice trembling with fear and exhaustion.

"Yes," Mia replied, keeping her voice calm and steady. "I can hear you. What happened?"

"I got separated from my mom," the pup said, its voice cracking. "The tide pulled me away, and I… I'm so tired. I don't know where to go."

Mia's heart clenched. She inched closer, her movements slow and careful. "It's okay," she said gently. "You're safe now. We're going to help you."

Luke crouched beside her; his face etched with concern. "What's it saying?"

Mia glanced at him. "It's scared and exhausted. It got separated from its mom and hasn't been able to rest or find food. It's dehydrated too." She pointed to the pup's dry, cracked skin.

Luke nodded grimly. "We'll call the Marine Mammal Center. This little one needs professional care."

The pup let out a weak whimper, trying to shuffle away but collapsing again. Mia moved closer, her voice soothing. "Don't move too much. Save your energy." She reached out her hand slowly, letting the pup sniff her fingers before gently stroking its fur. "You're really brave," she whispered.

The pup sniffled, its big eyes brimming with tears. "Will it hurt?"

"No," Mia said firmly. "The people at the center are going to help you feel better. I promise."

Luke asked Mia for her handheld VHF marine radio, then he set it to Channel 16 to call for help. He knew there was no cellphone service on this rural area of the coast. "This is Pitter Patter anchored off Año Nuevo," he said into the handset. "We've got an injured elephant seal pup on the beach—dehydrated, weak, and in need of medical attention. Requesting assistance from the Marine Mammal Center."

A crackling response came through. "Pitter Patter, this is the U.S. Coast Guard Sector San Francisco. We'll notify the Marine Mammal Center and send someone out. Stand by."

Mia stayed with the pup, stroking its fur gently as it whimpered. "You're not alone," she said softly. "I'm right here."

The pup closed its eyes briefly, as if comforted by her presence. "Thank you," it whispered.

About an hour later, a white truck from the Marine Mammal Center pulled onto the beach. A woman with dark hair tied back in a ponytail climbed out, then got out a large animal crate from the back of the truck. She waved as she approached.

"Hi, I'm Carolina," she said warmly. "Thanks for calling this in."

Mia stood and gestured toward the pup. "It's really scared," she explained. "I've been talking to it to keep it calm, but it's really weak and hasn't had any food or water."

Carolina knelt beside the pup, her face full of compassion as she examined it. "You did a great job keeping it calm," she said. "This pup is definitely dehydrated, and it's showing signs of malnutrition.

We need to get it back to the center as soon as possible for fluids and care."

Carolina opened the crate and placed it gently on the sand, but the pup immediately started to panic.

"No! I don't want to go!" it cried, thrashing weakly.

Mia knelt down beside it, speaking softly. "It's okay," she said. "This crate will take you to people who can help, I promise."

The pup hesitated, its body trembling. "Will it hurt?" "No," Mia reassured it. "It'll feel strange at first, but once you're at the center, they'll make sure you feel better."

The pup looked at her, its eyes wide with trust. "Okay… if you'll visit me soon."

"Of course," Mia said, stroking its head gently.

With Carolina's help, Mia carefully guided the pup into the crate. The pup whimpered but stayed still, keeping its eyes on Mia the entire time. Once the door was secured, Carolina stood and nodded.

"Great job," Carolina said. "This little one's in good hands now. We'll take it back to the center, give it fluids, and monitor its health. If everything goes well, we'll release it back here in a few weeks."

Mia's face lit up. "Can I come visit it at the center?"

"Absolutely," Carolina said with a smile. "In fact, why don't you come for a tour? I'd love to show you what we do."

"I'd love that!" Mia said, her excitement bubbling over.

As the truck drove away, Mia stood with her dad, watching until it disappeared over the dunes. She turned to him, her heart full.

"That felt… amazing," she said.

Luke placed a hand on her shoulder. "You've got a gift, Mia. And you're using it to make a real difference."

Mia looked out at the sparkling waves. The ocean held so many challenges, but she was ready for all of them.

Get your copy of

Mia Kingtide :

Guardian of the Coast

to read the rest of the story

Available at

PITTERPATTERDIVING.COM

About the Author

Luke Kilpatrick, based in Sand City along California's stunning Pacific Coast, is a passionate storyteller and explorer of all things California. His books delve into the beauty, culture, and spirit of the coastal regions and the Golden State at large. An avid scuba diver, photographer, surfer, and boater, Luke brings his deep connection to the ocean and outdoors to life in his writing and his puzzle books.

With a career that began in graphic design and software development, Luke transitioned to developer marketing and relations, where he's excelled for over 15 years. When he's not crafting stories or navigating the tech world, he manages The Ocean View at Monterey Bay, a charming vacation rental where guests are invited to take his books home as a memento of their stay. Luke's love for California shines through in his work, blending his talents and passions to celebrate the state's unparalleled landscapes and lifestyle.

Connect with Luke:
Website: www.pitterpatterdiving.com
Twitter: @lkilpatrick
Facebook: facebook.com/lukekilpatrick
TikTok: PitterPatterDiving

www.ingramcontent.com/pod-product-compliance
Lightning Source LLC
LaVergne TN
LVHW010929110826
845149LV00013B/2526